FOR THE LOVE OF DANCE

BY

J D Baird

Approximately 44,000 words

Cover design by Adam Howie © 2022

J D Baird © 2022

Contents

Acknowledgements 4

Chapter 1- It's Hot In Here! 5

Chapter 2 - New Friends 13

Chapter 3 - Jealousy 32

Chapter 4 - Disaster At First Sight 40

Chapter 5 - Coffee 49

Chapter 6 - The Phonecall 57

Chapter 7 - Ice Cream And Dogs 63

Chapter 8 – He Cooks? 75

Chapter 9 – Sweet Surprises 90

Chapter 10 – Loose Ends 100

Chapter 11 – See You Tonight 107

Chapter 12 – Goodbye at The Duke 111

Chapter 13 – London's Calling 117

Chapter 14 – Meeting The Cast 125

J D Baird © 2022

Chapter 15 – I Love You 138

Chapter 16 – He Loves Me Too 144

Chapter 17 - I Miss Him 151

Chapter 18 – Sorry...162

Chapter 19 – Eric Calling 172

Chapter 20 – How Long?...180

Chapter 21 – Talk To Me...184

Chapter 22 – Food For Thought 189

Chapter 23 – First Night Nerves..202

Chapter 24 – Meet The Parents 212

Chapter 25 – Curtain Call 222

Chapter 26 – The Beginning Of An End 236

Chapter 27 – You Can't Smoke Down Here 241

Chapter 28 – I Can't Let You Go 245

Chapter 29 – Nightmare...249

Epilogue 251

J D Baird © 2022

ACKNOWLEDGEMENTS

I would like to say a huge thank you to all the people that read my story in its early stages, your feedback and encouragement was much appreciated.

Thank you to Mike, for listening to me read and hear the story change chapter by chapter.

Thank you to my children, Isabelle and Amber for your grammatical input and to Adam for designing the cover, just as I imagined. I lu! x

J D Baird © 2022

CHAPTER 1- IT'S HOT IN HERE!

I am incredibly nervous but the boy across the room, with the dark curly hair and the most delicate smile, suppresses my nerves. I just cannot take my eyes off him. He looks right at me, I'm sure of it. My heart almost comes out of my mouth, and I feel something flip in my gut. He's perfect. I quickly run a hand through my quiff and shake my hair from side to side. I look down at my hands then crack each finger in turn, intertwine my fingers and stretch out my arms in front of me. My palms are sweaty, and my hands begin to shake, I press a thumb into each palm in turn, clench my hands into fists before stretching out my fingers.

J D Baird © 2022

I am sitting in a holding room with the other dancers, waiting to audition; it is warm and uncomfortable, but there's a breeze from the open door which is friendly and welcoming. My choice of outfit helps to keep me cool too, a white cotton vest and black dance leggings.

I came alone today but I know mum would have wanted to be here, I know she would have been right by my side. She always said I had talent, she said I would go far, let's hope her premonitions are proved right today. I feel her soothing presence looking down on me.

Next to him, is a rather pretty woman, who I presume must be his mum, she has the same deep, thick, curly hair. She looks at him with immense pride. I look too, he's wearing black dance trousers and a black vest, an assortment of tattoos drawn down his arms, black looks good on him. I stare as he takes a sip of water, they talk and laugh together. A young man appears at the door to the audition room and calls out a name.

"Ben, Ben Thomas, you're up next."

J D Baird © 2022

He stands up, he's tall, maybe 6'2, I can't be sure. The proud woman kisses his forehead and wishes him luck, he turns to leave the room but right before he goes through the door, he turns to me and smiles softly. His gaze locking mine, holding me in a trance. His eyes are as deep and green as the ocean, I could swim in them for hours. *'Come on Daniel!'* I tell myself, *'He is the competition.'*

I play around with the zip of my bag nervously and go through the routine counts in my head. The first part just doesn't feel quite right, and I can't get that left foot turn into the leap. I wonder if I should take it out. *'Could it be too late to change the steps?'* The judges will be looking for ambitious choreography, I'm sure of it. *'This is ambitious!'* It is by far the hardest routine I have ever performed. They will want to see confidence too. This is for a dream role in the West End. I know they are going to be looking for perfection. *'Perfection?'* I wonder how curls is doing, he's sure to be great, he just looks so professional. I can't change it now. *'Daniel, you can do this.'* I tell myself over and over.

J D Baird © 2022

I wish mum were here. I close my eyes for a second. I see her gentle face smiling at me. She's telling me I'm amazing, her eyes beaming with pride.

It's around thirty minutes before curls re-enters the room, he is glowing and looks chuffed. He wipes his forehead with a towel and bends forward, out of breath, beads of sweat trickle down his temple. I watch as he tells his mum what he did. His mum hugs him tight, before almost spinning him around.

"Mum!"

His voice is deep, but he is clearly embarrassed. I smirk and he catches me looking so I direct my eyes to the floor. I slowly look up and back to him, his gaze sweeps over me, can this be for real?

"Daniel Walters, we are ready for you… Daniel Walters?" "Daniel?"

Shit, that's me!

"I'm here!" I say, as I stand and hit the table with my knee.

J D Baird © 2022

Curls turns in my direction, fuck! I try to casually exit, but all the time curls looks right at me with eyes like lasers and it burns, I can feel the heat from him, pierce into my skin.

"Good luck!" he mouths towards me; a smile plays across his lips.

"Thank you!" I whisper back as I close the door behind me.

In the room, two people are sat at a desk with notepads, the nerves hit me hard, and I can feel my heart pounding in my chest, but I am unsure if this is from my brief encounter with the most beautiful man alive or if it is because the next few minutes determine the rest of my life.

"Good morning, Daniel, how are you?" questions the lady at the table.

She is smart looking but has a strict dance history demeanour about her.

"I'm good thank you, really good!" I lie through a fake smile.

I'm wobbling inside and I feel like I'm going to be sick.

"Which dance have you prepared?" asks the gentleman sitting next to her, as he shuffles around some paperwork before tapping it on the desk to straighten it out.

He is also smartly dressed, balding and slightly overweight. He looks as though he has never seen a dance floor before, let alone ever been on one.

I go through the routine I have arranged, and they wish me good luck, the music starts, and I begin. Curls clouds my judgement and concentration, as I go through the movements all I can think about is getting back into the holding room to say hi, wish him good luck (not that he needs it) and to, well… just see him again. Maybe we could go out for coffee? A beer? I'll ask him as soon as I'm through with this I think as I'm counting the beats in my head. 5, 6, 7, 8, leap, turn, twist, drop, 5, 6, 7, 8 run, 2, 3, 4, pause and finish. The music stops and I'm in my final pose. I drag myself back to reality. Did I hit the steps? My chest is rising and falling rapidly, I'm sure I haven't done enough, but as mum used to say, 'What will be, will be."

J D Baird © 2022

"Thank you, Daniel, you may wait in the holding room and a member of the team will be with you shortly." The man gestures towards the door.

'Brutal!' I thought as I made my way to the exit, no follow up questions or small talk, but that's just the way it is. There is tough competition in this game and it's not easy by any means.

As I head out, I scan the room for curls. He's gone! I am devastated. I look around again with hopeless desperation before slumping into the chair to put my shoes back on. In my misery, I see a card on the table, that definitely wasn't there beforehand – *a telephone number and a single X,* could it be? It must be!

As I'm ready to leave, one of the production runners heads my way and hands me a form to sign.

"Daniel, you were meant to take this before leaving the room."

I scan the white piece of paper quickly, my eyes glazing across the words from top to bottom, and sign; he informs me that they are extremely busy, but I should receive a call back by 5pm

J D Baird © 2022

this evening. I head out into the humid, packed streets and look for the nearest air-conditioned cafe.

J D Baird © 2022

CHAPTER 2 - NEW FRIENDS

"Call him, you fool!" screams Stella from her room.

"And say what exactly?"

Stella is my flatmate, we have been friends since college, she is extreme, but I love her. She has so many crazy quirks about her, she is the most beautiful girl I know and quite frankly, I tend to *not* find girls attractive, but she has a heart of gold and would do anything to see others happy. I simply would not survive in this world without her. Since losing mum, she has been my rock, through the crying and the heart ache, she has pulled me through. This girl has quite literally saved my life.

"Tell him you love him; tell him you need him," she sings entering the room in her hungover state. Hair in pigtails, oversized t-shirt and pants, white football socks up to her knees and she's clutching a bottle of water.

"It might not even be him," I wonder.

She flumps down, right beside me and swipes the card from my hand and studies it.

"But who else would leave a number with no name, in the place you were sat? Checking out any other hot guys were you?" she teases as she turns the card over.

"Hey Dan, what's this?"

I look at the card.

70's Theme Night

The Old Duke

Friday 9pm til' late

"This is tonight!" she squeals with excitement, "Let's go!"

Even if I wanted to say no, I had no choice in the matter. Stella grabs two beers from the fridge, I really don't know how she is able to drink after pretty much just getting up from the night before and she shoves one into my hand.

"Cheers!" Stella taps my bottle enthusiastically.

"Cheers!" I reply, with an air of resistance.

J D Baird © 2022

After a second bottle, we dance around the place throwing out shapes to a 70's playlist, whilst changing numerous outfits until we come up with the perfect collaboration of materials. Stella has teamed a blue and white A-line dress with bell sleeves and white knee-high boots, she has scraped her hair on top of her head, into what resembles a beehive and I'm wearing a pair of Stella's black, flared trousers and a golden-brown, weirdly coloured metallic shirt, with the buttons undone to my belly button. To complete the outfit, Stella has sharpied above my lip, an authentic 1970's moustache. We both fall about laughing as I see it in the mirror.

"Drink up, the Uber is arriving," Stella yells, above the music.

***

As we pull up to The Duke, there is a steady queue forming, with so many outfits on show. Afros here and there. Girls all in high boots. Satin and flares. I'm not the only one with a tash, but I think I may be the only one with a permanent marker style tash. Considering I was hesitant, this is going to be so much fun!

J D Baird © 2022

When we get inside, we head upstairs to the function room, it is decorated with disco balls and coloured lights. Bearing in mind there is a bog-standard pub downstairs, the upstairs has been astoundingly transformed. Without charging an entry fee, The Duke's budget has stretched to display some extreme 70's memorabilia. Next to the bar, is a life-size cut out of 'The Fonz' and in the corner is a bright orange egg chair. It could almost have the residual energy of the actual 70's up here. The bar is old, but functional, to the left of the room is a balcony which has been made into an outside seating area. Just the thing for this time of year. The air is humid, but the atmosphere is electric.

"Two beers, please and four shots," Stella politely asks the girl behind the bar, who is dressed up in a black and white mini-dress and blonde bobbed wig. She almost looks like a chess board, but she looks amazing! Stella picks up a pint and is about to pass it to me before she is nudged from the side and the pint almost goes flying my way.

"What the hell are you doing?" she screams as she shoves the cold, wet glass into my hand.

J D Baird © 2022

"It was a fucking accident, you idiot!" comes the response.

"Calm down girls!" pleads the girl on the bar.

"Me?" asks Stella bluntly, as she taps her card on the reader and tuts loudly.

"Four shots?" I question. This is going to be one of those nights! We down a shot at the bar and head outside.

We go out onto the balcony and Stella hands me a cigarette.

"Did you see that?" she asks, bewildered.

"I did," I laugh, "but I'm sure she didn't mean it," I pause to light my cigarette, "sometimes Stella, you need to think before you act," I continue.

"Yea, yea Daniel, we're not all as sensible as you are, Mr I will take a week thinking about something before making a decision. The guy who counts the pockets on trousers before buying."

"Hey!" I laugh, "I'm not that bad and that was one time Stella, and in my defence, three pockets just weren't enough."

"Blah, blah, blah, now drink up!"

J D Baird © 2022

Stella sinks her second shot and I follow suit. The sharp tang makes me shudder, so I sip my pint to balance the taste.

The music is blaring, and the night is so young. Bohemian Rhapsody begins to play, Stella squeals impatiently as she grabs me by the arm and hurries inside to the dance floor. She pulls me by the hand towards the flashes of square lights, anyone would think *she* was the professional dancer.

Come to think of it, I hadn't heard anything from the audition today, they said they would call back by the end of the day. I take my phone from the pocket of Stella's flared jeans in anticipation to check I haven't missed anything, nope absolutely nothing! I can't help but feel disappointed. Stella senses the rejection in my body language.

"Ahh well!" she scolds as she takes my phone from my hand and puts it swiftly into her bag, "All the more reason to get pissed tonight!" she laughs as she twirls me around the dance floor.

We continue to bop around to another few familiar hits, we point our thumbs from left to right and hold our noses as we pretend to swim. We criss-cross our arms on top of each other, in some kind of slicing motion. Apparently, these were the popular moves back in the day. If anything, it is fun. 'Night Fever' begins to play, and the dance floor fills up.

"Bernie!" Stella cries out, as two girls push their way through the crowd.

"Oh my gosh, Stella! How are you?" asks the taller girl of the two.

"I'm great," replies Stella excitedly and she introduces us. "Dan, meet Bernie, Bernie, meet Dan. Dan, this is my really good friend from high school, she left after year 11 and I haven't seen her since!"

The girls hug and scream at each other, they begin talking, jumping up and down in sync and reminiscing old times. The other girl joins in the conversation. I look at Stella, she is just so happy.

"I'll get a round in," I exclaim and take the drink orders from them.

I stroll over to the bar with a smile on my face. Stella is just the best, I think to myself.

J D Baird © 2022

There's a small queue at the bar but that's not a problem, I need the distraction from the contrast of Stella's happiness and my own thoughts of yet another failed audition. I place my order and feel around in my pockets for my phone, it wouldn't hurt to check again would it? I wonder if I have any missed calls or messages. Damn, Stella has my phone.

"I'll just be a sec," I signal to the girl on the bar and head back over to Stella.

She hands me my phone reluctantly, with a face full of pity.

"That doesn't help," I sigh, and I walk back over to the bar with my head down tapping in my pin code. I look up and two of the drinks are made, I look back to my phone and open WhatsApp.

"Calling me, I hope?"

I hear a deep voice - it can't be. I look up. Bright green eyes staring back at me.

"Curls!" I blurt out, "umm, I mean, hi!"

'Have I just called him curls? To his face?' I flush with embarrassment and the butterflies begin to panic in my stomach.

"That will be £12.80!" said the girl on the bar.

J D Baird © 2022

"I've got this!" says…, shit, what was his name? "Can you add an extra pint to that please, and two shots?"

"Thank you!" I respond, dumbstruck.

He pays and hands me a shot.

"Cheers!" he says as he holds up the bright green liquid in front of my face.

"Cheers!" I respond, not quite believing my eyes.

We bang the glasses on the bar in sync and he hands me three of the pints and follows me to the dance floor with the other two. I hold the drinks in a triangle, scared stiff that one will drop at any moment, petrified to turn around. I walk slow and it feels like forever to get back. The girls are wrapped up, still deep in conversation. I stand in front of Stella trying my best to nod my head in a backwards motion without getting caught but she doesn't notice, and she eases one of the pints from my hands and I pass the others to Bernie and her friend.

Curls hands me my pint and Stella looks at me, eyes wide open and eyebrows raised as though they were the McDonald's arches!

J D Baird © 2022

"We. Shall. Talk. Later!" she commands as she moves her finger to and fro, from me to…. him? *'What the fuck is his name?'* He smiles at her, then at me. He nods to the others, and they smile back. Oh man, this is awkward.

"Let's go outside." says…

"Ben!" he said quickly, as if reading my mind, I try to answer but my mouth doesn't work.

He leads the way outside and takes the table closest to the door, he puts his pint down, wipes his hand on his trousers and lights up a cigarette. He shakes my hand.

"Nice to meet you…," he waits. "properly."

I smile and sip my pint. My throat is dry.

"Hi!" is all I can manage.

He sits down and I sit too.

Curls, umm... Ben is wearing brown flares and a blue and orange striped shirt. He looks so good. I blink as I take a large gulp of my pint. He has a silver ring on his right thumb which glistens in the light every time he lifts his glass. His hair meanders across his face and he sweeps it away with the palm of his hand. His shoulders are broad, and his physique is fit, which boasts from underneath his tight shirt pushing hard against the fabric. '*He should unbutton it.*' I think to myself and realise I'm staring. I sit up quickly and drink.

"So how did your audition go today?" he asks with a smile.

"Well, I'm really not sure," I respond, "they haven't called back."

"Oh? That's odd," he says as he screws up his eyebrows then sticks out his bottom lip in thought whilst looking directly into my eyes.

I blink and look away. Then back at him. He takes a puff of his cigarette, which he holds between his thumb and index finger, then he throws it to the floor and stamps it out.

"I really should give up."

"How about you? I ask, "You seemed quite pleased when you came out."

"Watching me, were you?" Ben chuckled playfully as he nudged my arm.

"No, I… Well, yes. Yes, I was," I admit, "but back to you. How did it go?"

"They gave me the role of Matthew," Ben says trying his best to hold in his delight.

"That is fucking impressive!" I reply with genuine elation.

Matthew was the lead part in the show, so it came as no surprise; Matthew's character was supposedly a heart throb and Ben is that for sure. Dancer or not, he's won me over.

"It is impressive, isn't it?" That's half of why I'm celebrating tonight, we were going to come here anyway."

"We?" I ask.

"Oh yes, I'm sorry, it's one of my housemates' birthdays tonight and we were coming out for that, but they are not here yet and I came straight from my mum's house.

'Hold it together Dan!' I think to myself as his deep tone, penetrates through my body as he speaks.

"They are pretty late actually, no doubt the pre-drinks went on a bit."

"Was that your mum at the audition?" I query, diverting from the fact he would soon be leaving with friends.

"Yes, she has supported me since I started dancing, in fact it was her being pushy that got me to where I am now. She's my biggest fan," he beams.

"I'm so pleased for you. Does that mean you will be moving down to London when they start rehearsals?"

"Yes, I'd like to say unfortunately but I'm so excited. haven't found a place to stay yet, but that will all be sorted in time."

I hear a noise and look in through the door, Stella and friends were dancing to Dancing Queen, I was sure I could hear her raspy voice sailing above the music, singing along, and not in tune.

"Girlfriend?" quipped Ben.

"God no!" I shot back, in surprise.

"I'm only winding you up," sneered Ben. "I know *she's* not your type."

"She's not but she is my best friend, losing her would be like losing a piece of my heart."

"Drink?" Ben asks, changing the subject and drinking the remains of his pint, "Your round I believe?"

"Yes, absolutely!" I respond quickly, picking up our empty glasses from the table.

We stand up to leave and my pocket rings. I pass the glasses to Ben and answer my phone.

"Hello, Daniel speaking!"

"Ahh Daniel," I could hear Ben whisper, "you never did tell me your name."

He smiles and I smile back whilst listening to the speaker on the other end.

"Hi Daniel, sorry to call so late, it's Amanda Greenfield from Dance Stars Production Agency. Is this a good time to speak?"

"Yes, it's fine." I put a finger to my ear, to hear better, I was ready for the bad news; nothing could get me down from this high.

J D Baird © 2022

"It has been super busy here in the office and we haven't got round to calling everyone back yet. I wanted to call to give you feedback from this morning."

"Okay?" I say in a low tone, as I roll my eyes at Ben.

I notice he's looking right at me, studying me and has been since I answered the phone. I take a deep breath.

"Your audition was incredible, and you are a very strong applicant," I hear the voice say on the other end. I can feel my breathing become heavier. "We are offering you the part of Elijah. Would you be willing to accept?"

I sit down, "Wow! Umm, yes! Wow! Thank you! Oh my gosh! Yes!" I respond, without hesitation.

"We shall take that as firm acceptance then Daniel. We have your details on file and will forward the paperwork and dates to you in the morning. Congratulations, we are really looking forward to working with you!"

"Thank you so much," I gasp.

It's our pleasure, goodbye."

J D Baird © 2022

"Goodbye." I press the red end call button and look up at Ben, he is still standing, smoking. I can't help but stare.

"Well?" he asks, "Sounds like good news?"

"Elijah," I respond, "they have offered me the part of Elijah!"

"Fuck me," Ben laughs, "that's freaking amazing. Triple celebrations tonight then. Oh, and you do realise you will have no choice but to kiss me? It's a part of the performance after all."

"Wow, yes! I must tell Stella! And as for kissing you, it would have happened anyway, right?"

I was clearly drunk now, those shots had hit hard, there's no way I would have said that in the real world. There was just something about Ben that made me feel alive.

We head inside, could this night get any better?

"Drake man, what's happened to you?" Ben calls out as he clocks his friends, three of them.

The birthday boy was already a little worse for wear. What looked like it had started out as a great outfit was now a mess. Half of his shirt tucked in, half out. He had a large badge pinned to the front of him and colourful streamers in his hair. Eric, a tall, handsome man with blonde hair goes to give Ben a hug, and Ben sharply reaches out to Sid and tugs on his shirt.

"This looks amazing!" he says diverting the embrace.

Eric looks at me and I feel uneasy. Sid looks slightly younger than the others, a pretty face, huge grin and messy hair.

"So, how did today go?" Sid asks Ben.

I leave Ben with his friends as I go to find Stella. As I walk away, Ben's hand brushes against mine which makes me shiver, I look up at him. He smiles then turns back towards his friends.

Stella and I sit at a vacant table, and I tell her the good news. I watch the dancefloor. I can see Bernie's friend kissing, what looks like one of the guys that had come to meet Ben. I squint my eyes, and shrug. I look back at Stella.

"Your mum would be so proud Dan!" she smiles at me, "tonight, let's raise a glass to her."

I go to get drinks, a second time and meet Bernie at the bar.

"Your friend isn't shy!" I quip.

She helps me walk back to the table where Stella has been joined by Ben, the birthday boy, and Eric. On the count of three, we all down a shot.

"We should hit the town!" announces Bernie suddenly, "I'm up for going out, out."

Her friend Chloe agrees as she emerges, bumping into the table, Sid steadies her.

"Why, thank you." she slurs and kisses him.

"Ben, we should get and early night," Eric gestures, putting a hand on Ben's knee, "I can call an Uber."

A pang of jealousy hits me hard in the chest. Oh no, he was taken, which would mean he was a player. Which would also mean, I really had made a fool of myself.

"No Eric, the night is just getting started, and we are celebrating," responds Ben, removing Eric's hand from his leg. "You go back to the house, and maybe take Drake back, he looks like he needs to sleep."

Stella also saw this and raised her eyebrows in my direction.

J D Baird © 2022

"Sid and I will take Drake home," said Chloe. "We're pretty tired," she said, laughing into Sid's shoulder.

"That's that then!" confirms Ben. "Eric, how about you?"

"Looks like I will have to accompany you to town then." Eric seems infuriated and quite clearly has history with Ben. Ben shakes his head and smiles in my direction.

We finish our drinks, and the girls go to use the bathroom together. Sid makes conversation with me whilst Ben and Eric talk to each other near the door. The conversation looks fractured, Eric tries to put a hand on Ben's shoulder and Ben steps backwards.

"Are they ok?" I ask Sid.

He's about to answer and the girls return, we stagger downstairs, out of the door and disperse into separate Ubers. Chloe and Sid leave in one with Drake. I sit in between Ben and Eric in the back of another and Bernie and Stella go in the third, how I wish I was sitting between Bernie and Stella.

J D Baird © 2022

CHAPTER 3 - JEALOUSY

"Eric it is an audition, it is important to me!"

I had spent the night with him once and now he just won't leave me alone.

"Ben, but this will mean a move to London and what will that mean for us?" Eric mumbles.

"Us?" I ask him, impatiently. "There is no us!"

"I mean our friendship, Ben. The fact that we share a house together," he lies, trying to put a hand on my shoulder.

"You know that's not what you meant Eric."

I was really annoyed now, why was he being like this? I brush his hand away and walk to the front door. I grab my keys out of the bowl, he just stands there in the doorway looking right at me.

"Now, I must go, I'll meet you at the party later and we can talk when we get home tonight," I tell him. "Wish me luck?" I ask, opening the door.

J D Baird © 2022

"Good luck, Ben," he responds quietly and walks back towards the kitchen.

I close the door and leave.

It is inhumanely hot outside, I put my shades on and jump into the passenger side of mum's car.

"You ok, love?" she asks sweetly.

"I'm fine mum!" I say kissing her cheek and putting my seatbelt on.

"You look tense," she notes as she pulls away.

"Just nerves, I guess," I tell her, rubbing the sides of my temple with my fingers.

***

We arrive at the venue, and I sign in. We sit in a holding room and mum just won't stop fussing. She keeps asking me questions and touching my hair. I'm trying my best to look cool, especially after I see this gorgeous lad sat alone, and he's checking me out. He's *very* cute but he looks quite nervous, almost shy. However, I have never known a dancer to hide from the limelight. I think about going to say hello, there's something about him which I find fascinating, intriguing almost, aside from the fact he is totally hot, there is something mysterious about him. *'No.'* I tell myself; I need to keep a clear head. This is the most important day in my life so far and distractions from pretty boys are not what I need right now.

"You should go and say hi!" says mum. "He looks ever so lonely," she adds, and we laugh.

I drink my water to stop me from laughing even more. Mum can be funny sometimes.

My name is called out and I stand up quickly, I drag myself back to reality, I am here to dance, mum kisses me on the head to wish me luck, I take a deep breath and I go in.

When I return, mum is waiting eagerly and wide-eyed. I tell her that I think it went really well and I was proud of what I had done; I was sure I had done the best I could. Out of nowhere, mum squeezes me tightly and tries to spin me around. I'm mortified. I hear cute boy laugh and I look over, he quickly puts his head down, but it pleases me to know he's watching. He looks back up and I smile straight at him. We hold eye contact for a moment, the most electrifying, terrifying moment that sets my heart ablaze.

I turn back to mum as I hear her talking down the phone to dad. She lets him know we will be leaving soon. A name is called, and he stands up, I turn and watch him leave, my eyes drawn to him like magnets, wondering if I should wait.

"Good luck!" I mouth to him, and he reads my lips.

"Thank you!" he whispers right back, closing the door and stopping my heart at the same time.

The producers told me they would contact me if I was successful, so there was nothing left to do here. I change and put my shoes back on.

"You ready to go?" asks mum.

"Yea, one sec," I say as I scramble around in my jeans pocket for a scrap of paper to leave my number on.

I really need to see this guy again. He is beautiful.

I pull out a card from my back pocket and scribble on the back. I leave it on the table where he was sat, in the hope that he will call me before tonight. That way, maybe I could make my excuses to Eric and the others and not attend the 70's night after all.

Mum pulls the car up on the drive and dad is waiting on the doorstep, arms folded waiting for news.

"How did it go son?" he asks with eager anticipation.

"Pretty good, dad. I didn't miss a step," I continue to relay the audition to dad as we move inside the house.

"Well done lad!" he beams with happiness.

I can tell by his voice; he is immensely proud of me, and this makes me feel amazing inside.

I spend the rest of the afternoon at mums, I chill out in my old room and listen to music for a while before having dinner. I check my phone multiple times before even thinking about getting ready, it was a long shot leaving my number, but I had to try. Nothing. Well, apart from the four missed calls and seven WhatsApp messages from Eric, that I haven't opened.

I open them.

'Good luck today, remember you're amazing. I'm sorry about earlier x.'

'Looking forward to tonight x.'

'See you later! xx'

'Call me when you get my messages!'

'Ben?'

'Ben, I'm getting worried now.'

'Fine, maybe I shouldn't come tonight? If that's what u want?'

I call him.

"Hi Ben!" he answers on the first ring.

"Eric, what the fuck is wrong with you? You know exactly where I was."

"I was worried about you; how did the audition go?" he says desperately.

"You have no need to worry Eric, I am 24 years old, and the audition went great thank you. We can talk tonight; I already told you that," I tell him coldly.

He's really starting to piss me off and I really don't want to have this conversation with him any longer. There's silence.

"Ben, can I ask you something?" he stammers keenly.

"What is it?" I say with a loud sigh.

"Is there a chance for us?"

I laugh loudly, but I don't find any of this at all funny. "Eric, you know how I feel. It was one night, we were drunk. We're friends. That's it!"

What will it take for him to get the message?

"But…" he persists.

"No Eric, I shall see you soon. And please…"

"What?" he interrupts.

"Do not bring it up tonight," I plead.

I hang up the phone before he gets a chance to reply and toss it to the end of my bed. I close my eyes for a while and before long I feel myself drifting off to sleep. I wake up an hour or so later and sit on the end of my bed, yawn loudly and stretch my arms into the air. I reach to the bottom of my bed for my discarded phone, and I check for messages, missed calls. Nothing. I was really hoping he would call; I can't get him out of my mind. I place my phone on charge and I head to the shower, knowing full well I don't want to go tonight. I could quite easily avoid Eric for the rest of my life, but Drake is one of my best friends and I really don't want to let him down.

I shower, get dressed and head downstairs for food. Dad has lent me one of his old shirts, it looks great and it's an original 70's print.

"You look lovely, just like your dad," mum coos as she looks over to him and he puts his hand on hers across the table.

It really is nice to come back home occasionally and sit down to eat with my parents, it reminds me of simpler times.

"Do you want a lift to the pub?" asks mum, releasing her hands from dad's and standing up to clear the table.

"No thank you, it's a warm night, I'll walk," I reply.

Mum is just the sweetest creature, but I really could do with the air, and I need to practice what I'm going to say to Eric later. No matter how I say it. He's not going to like what I have to say.

CHAPTER 4 - DISASTER AT FIRST SIGHT

I walk into the pub and it's in full swing. The music is loud and upbeat, the atmosphere is joyful and merry, the dance floor is full, the bar is heaving, and the drinks are flowing. I look around the room, there's bright costumes everywhere, no effort has been spared. Such a variety of people are out and enjoying the night. I see no sign of my friends yet, so I go straight over to the bar to order a well-deserved pint. I see a familiar face, *Fuck! No way! It can't be. He's here?* I squint my eyes to make sure. Shit, act cool Ben. The boy from this morning is standing by the bar, just inches away. I ease my way to the side of him, not really knowing what I'm about to say. I try to compose myself before saying something stupid, which consequently doesn't work. He looks down at his phone and swipes a couple of times.

"Calling me?" I ask him casually but dying inside.

He looks up, startled, and utters something. Did he just call me '*curls*?'

I buy the round of drinks, half of which we take to his friends on the dance floor, and we go outside. He is definitely more handsome than I remember from this morning. He takes my breath away. His choice of outfit suits him, he looks unbelievably good but I'm not sure about the moustache, which I fear he's forgotten is there.

We sit outside and talk for a while, he seems nervous. Much the opposite to his friend inside, Stella. We talk about the audition this morning and I can't help but look at him and smile. Flirting with him is easy, I feel so comfortable in his company.

His phone rings and I find out his name is Daniel; I couldn't quite remember from the audition. Cute name though.

He looks stunned as he answers his phone, and he passes me our empty glasses. I look him up and down, whilst he talks on the phone. I urge to touch him. By his awkward expression, it's an important call so I light a cigarette and watch him intriguingly as I wait patiently.

He's very attractive, not typically handsome, but exceedingly alluring. He has a slim build, he's around six feet, well he's slightly shorter than me so I'm guessing, he has deep brown eyes, and gorgeous cheek bones. He catches me looking so I blink and look away.

Daniel ends the call and I find out he will be playing opposite me in the show.

"We will kiss!" I tell him, an air of mischief in my voice.

Joking aside, I want to kiss him now. He's breath-taking, the physical attraction I feel towards him is explosive. From his response, I can tell he wants to kiss me too. I'm not sure I've ever felt like this before, it's like he's put me under a spell.

We head back inside, and I see that my friends have arrived. Drake is a little worse for wear and Eric hasn't taken his eyes off me. He tries to hug me. This makes me feel uncomfortable, actually I'm quite annoyed with him. What is his problem?

Daniel introduces me to his friends, they seem really nice, and my friend Sid quickly makes friends with Stella's friend of a friend, Chloe. We sit, drink some more and one of Stella's friends

J D Baird © 2022

suggests we go into town. At this moment I'm keen to go wherever Daniel does.

Eric puts his hand on my leg, and asks me to leave with him, which repulses me, and I know that Daniel noticed this. I really hope he doesn't get the wrong impression, that's not who I am.

The girls head to the toilets and I speak with Eric by the door, whilst we wait.

"Eric, you have to let this go!" I sigh, forgetting what I had practised to say.

"But I like you, I know you like me too," he responds, moving his hand to my shoulder.

I push him away. I feel Daniel watching me, but I don't want to look over, instead I try to talk Eric into having a good night.

"Look Eric, we are really good friends," I force out my words. "Let's talk back at the house tonight."

He doesn't seem convinced. The group join us, and we head down the stairs. We all end up going into town together, minus Chloe and Sid, who find an ideal opportunity to leave by taking Drake home. I share an Uber with Eric and Daniel and it is by far the worst situation I have ever been in. I feel the awkwardness Daniel must feel, sat in between Eric and me.

I'm not sure what the club is called but the music is good. I feel the alcohol run through my veins giving me the confidence to make a move on Daniel. He's on the dancefloor with Stella so I begin to make my way over, however, Eric insisted we talk again. I try to tell him this isn't the time, but he is adamant he is going to get his way, so I let him. We sit at a table and talk. I'd had enough. The move to London really couldn't come sooner.

"Slow down, Eric!" I shout over the music. "You are drinking far too much."

"I'm not?" he responds, "I'm drowning my sorrows, what's your problem, Ben? I'm not your problem, why do you care?" he slurs.

"I don't!" I mutter to myself.

"Do you know how it feels to watch you drool over a man you just met? You hardly know him, and what is so special about him?" he rants on.

"Eric, I'm not drooling, and anyway, we are not together, I don't want you, I never did. It was a stupid mistake!" I tell him angrily. "I'm sorry, Eric," I apologise, feeling guilty from my outburst. "You just feel this way because you're drinking too, we've both drank too much. Eric, we can talk better in the morning," I reassure him with a lie.

I don't want to have this conversation again.

"Let's go home Ben, I love you. I know you feel something too," he begs.

"You're drunk, Eric. I'm not doing this with you, not now, I told you we would talk in the morning!" I snap again.

"Fine, be that way!" Eric snaps back and tips back his pint.

I leave Eric at the table and head to the dance floor to find Daniel. I'm outraged but I know I should really get Eric home; he's going to end up doing something stupid.

J D Baird © 2022

As I head over, I can see Daniel, he is dancing with Bernie, Stella is at the bar. He looks so happy, so beautiful. I take a large breath as I feel my head fuzz. I join them both and they smile at me and gesture for me to dance. I dance for a moment but think about Eric sat at the table alone.

As the music changes, I try to tell Daniel that I should leave but he can't hear me. I get close and shout in his ear. Being so close to him sends a shiver down my spine. He smells of cigarettes and alcohol, his hair is a mess, but his ridiculous moustache is still perfect. He still can't hear me. He moves my head to the side and shouts back into my ear. The touch of his hands on my face and his warm breath by my neck makes me close my eyes as he speaks. He turns my head back and we are face to face. We are very close. My lips are so close to his. He looks at me. I can't help but bite my bottom lip. Should I kiss him? He removes his hands from my face.

"I can't hear you!" he says as he tries to sign with his hands.

J D Baird © 2022

He's funny. I feel a tingle in my stomach. I really hope this isn't the last time I see him.

"I need to leave!" I shout, grasping both of his hands and pulling him closer.

I feel an instant connection between us, through the interlocking of our fingers. He must feel it too. It's strong enough for the whole club to feel it. He leans into me.

"Why?" he whispers close to my lips.

I edge closer, and closer, his eyes haven't left mine and our lips almost touch.

"Because…" I say, looking down at his lips, I can feel the warmth of his body against mine, he tightens the grip of my hands in his, I watch as he closes his eyes and I close mine, our lips touch…

"BEN!" I hear a scream!

I jump and turn suddenly to the direction of the noise. The music stops and Stella is running our way. Daniel lets go of my hands and instantaneously I feel cold.

"Ben, Ben…It's Eric. He's…" Stella wails.

J D Baird © 2022

I don't wait for the end of that sentence and rush over to where I left him, I fight my way through a sea of bodies, a drink is spilt down my dad's shirt and I rub my hand against the wet patch. I look up, he's not sat at the table anymore, there's a noisy crowd around him and I push my way through. He's lied on the floor with blood oozing from his left arm. There's a smashed pint glass on the table and a piece of it in his other hand.

"Ben, you came," he says as he closes his eyes, and the bloodied shard drops from his hand.

"Fuck!" I sigh.

I feel a hand on my shoulder. It is Daniel. I turn to him and our eyes lock. The almost kiss feels a million miles away now. My body aches for him.

"I have to go with him," I whisper.

The words barley leave my lips as Daniel responds.

"I know, he needs you!" he says as Stella puts an arm around him and rests her head on his shoulder.

"And I need you," I mutter under my breath as my attention returns to Eric.

J D Baird © 2022

CHAPTER 5 - COFFEE

It's been three days since I last saw Ben. I've hardly eaten or slept, worrying about a man I barely even know. I've thought about calling him, every second of every day, since the other night, but the longer I leave it, the harder it gets.

"What will you say when you finally pluck up the courage to talk to him?" asks Stella, as she walks in armed with two full cups of tea and a packet of biscuits.

She knows me so well.

"I really don't know," I sigh, staring at my phone. "Thank you for the tea!"

"My pleasure," she grins.

"He can't call me; it must be me. What is going on between them? Are they together? Maybe I'm getting into something which is incredibly too deep to handle?"

"You're over thinking!" says Stella, as she dunks a biscuit into her tea, bundles it into her mouth, whole, before making some rather disturbing slurping noises as she washes it down with the milky liquid she calls tea.

I'm pretty drama free really, if you don't count Stella that is. I tap in his number, It's now or never. How long is too long? I erase the digits. Maybe he's with Eric now. I tap in the digits again and leave them there on my phone.

"Just do it! For fuck's sake! If you don't I will!" urges Stella.

"Ok, ok!" I hit call! It's ringing, no turning back now.

"Hello?"

"Urm… Ben? Is that you?"

"Speaking!"

"Hi Ben, It's Daniel."

"Shit, Daniel, Hi!"

"Is this a bad time? I can call back later?" I panic, picturing him curled up with Eric, taking care of him, maybe even making him tea.

"No, no, it's absolutely fine, I was kind of hoping you would call… sooner."

"Yes, I wanted to, but I wasn't sure how you felt." *Or how I felt*, I thought to myself.

"Can we meet later?" he sprung on me.

"Umm, yes, I'd love to," I replied, knowing there was nothing I wanted more.

We arranged to meet at 4pm in the coffee shop on the high street.

"There you go!" smiles Stella. "How do you feel?"

"Pretty good," I smiled back and took a sip of tea.

"Not so bad after all, eh?" Stella gulped her tea until it was gone, and I respond silently.

***

It's 4.15pm and I sit alone, waiting for Ben. I'm having second thoughts and my stomach is in knots. I think about getting up to leave and the door swings open, he walks in and scans the room. He spots me, nods his head in my direction and strides over.

"Hey!"

"Hey!" I reply.

"Did you order?" he asks.

"No not yet."

"Ok, so what will it be?"

"Just a coffee, one sugar," I ask, and he heads to the counter "and milk!" I add as he leaves the table.

He turns back in my direction.

"Gotcha!"

I watch as he orders the drinks. He looks a little tired but so beautiful. He's wearing black denim skinny jeans and a black oversized hoody with a print on the back. His hair flops over his eyes as he talks to the person behind the counter, and he brushes it away. He heads back over to the table.

"So, what took so long?" he questions, as he sits down.

I tell him about how I wanted to call him right from the minute he left the club with Eric but how I was afraid of what his response might be.

He tells me about Eric and that he has gone to stay with his parents in Cornwall for a while. He explains how messed up Eric is, and he tells me about their recent night together. He says he hadn't realised just how into him Eric was and he swore that if he knew how he felt it would never have happened. He talks about how they had both been drinking, which they often did, as housemates but this time it went too far, and it just happened. He says how he has regretted every single minute of it, every single day. He explains how he's not that type of guy. I can hear in his voice that he really does regret it and it almost sounds like he is apologising to me.

The coffee arrives just at the right moment. I no longer wanted to hear about Eric, although I did feel a slight pang of sympathy for him. It must be tough loving someone and not have those feelings reciprocated. I have never been in love, or even close.

We both sit in silence for a while, sipping coffee and not really knowing what to say to one another. It's a weird silence, not awkward but confusing. I try to say something, and he does too. We laugh.

"You go," insists Ben.

I wasn't really sure what I was going to say.

"How does your mum feel about London?" I ask quickly.

"Well, she's actually quite pleased really. She's always supported my decisions. Same as my dad. How about you? Do you have family that will miss you? Mum? Dad?"

"I erm… I… Well, I… My… My mum's no longer around and dad, yea he's cool with it," I lie.

I hate my dad!

Now really wasn't the time to tell him about the night I walked in and found mum, overdosed in a pool of her own sick, surrounded by Vodka and painkillers, her lifeless body laid in front of me. Some memories are best left locked away. He doesn't question where my mum is, which is a relief. He just looks at me as though he is trying to read my thoughts. We finish the coffee and talk more about the upcoming performance.

"It's going to be crazy in London!" I exclaim.

"Absolutely!" Ben agrees.

The air falls silent. I look down at my empty cup and run my finger around the rim, not knowing what else to say now.

"Hey!" cries Ben suddenly. "Here's a random thought."

J D Baird © 2022

He studies me, looking deep into my eyes, trying to second guess my thoughts.

"Never mind," he retreats.

"What is it?" I ask.

"It's a bad idea, that's what it is," he replies.

Just say it, will you!" I urge.

"Let's live together in London!" he blasts, my mouth falls open in disbelief. "I know we have only just met like, but why the fuck not? We will be working so closely together; it just makes sense."

I am totally stunned with this suggestion but at the same time thrilled by it. I've never really been a spare of the moment type of guy but like Ben questioned. *'Why the fuck not?'*

"Ok. Bad idea?" utters Ben. "I said it was, just forget it."

I realise I haven't said a word, but I have mentally packed my bags and left for London, hand in hand with Ben.

"Yes! "I declare.

"Yes?" Ben looks at me wide-eyed.

J D Baird © 2022

"Let's do it! Let's actually do it!" I agree, surprising myself.

"Splendid!" he responds, grabbing both of my hands from across the table. "If we're going to live together, I will need your number," he chuckles.

'*Splendid indeed*!' I think to myself as he taps my number into his phone.

CHAPTER 6 - THE PHONECALL

I arrive back to the flat and Stella is on the phone to her sister, she looks livid. I go to my room, without asking any questions. As I stretch out on the bed, so many thoughts race through my mind. I try to remind myself that I am a quiet boy from Leeds and this week's events are far from normal. I sit up on the bed and look in the mirror, I see my mum, I rub a hand across my cheek, we definitely do have the same face. I look up to the ceiling and sigh, *'I know you are there mum, listening and watching, I hope I am making you proud.'*

Stella bursts into my room, I almost jump out of my skin, and she joins me on the bed.

"For fuck's sake Stella!"

She lies next to me, her petite frame filling the space. She puts her arms above her head and huffs loudly.

My eyes follow the cracks on the ceiling, and I visualise tiny rivers. I then begin to imagine small boats sailing along the imaginary mini rivers. At this point, Stella is just background noise. Something about her sister's husband cheating on her with a girl from the office.

"…and that's when she walked in, she went to meet him after work. They were alone in the office, he tried to talk his way out of it, but it was too late. Daniel! Are you even listening?"

"Yes!" I lie, I was trying to, but I had so many thoughts battling for my attention, mum, Ben, London, …the little boats…

"Want to get out of here?" Stella asks, sitting up promptly.

I didn't, so I politely turn her down.

"I'm not really in the mood for drinking tonight," I tell her softly.

"Ok babe! I'll leave you to it!" she responds.

"Thank you, Stella!"

She hugs me tight before heading out of my room, leaving my door ajar and I hear her on the phone.

"Bernie! Hey! Fancy a few drinks tonight?" The conversation trails off, so I stand and close the door.

When Stella leaves the flat falls eerily silent, I sit up on the edge of the bed. The only person I want to talk to right now is Ben.

I feel so good around him. I wonder if he feels the same. I stare at my wardrobe, and I contemplate organising it ready for London. Instead, I lay back onto the pillow and close my eyes. I picture Ben and the way his hair falls across his face. I imagine what the kiss may have felt like had it happened that night… I'm drifting off to sleep when I hear my phone buzz. *'What fresh hell has she got herself into now?'* I ponder. I begrudgingly look at my phone. Ben!

"Hello?"

"Hi Daniel, I just had to call. I couldn't stop thinking about you!" he blurts out.

"Wow! Ben, I, umm I, I actually feel the same, I have been thinking about you all day."

"So, what does this mean?" he asks.

"I really don't know. I mean, I know you make me smile when you're around," I answer with all honesty.

"I know something," he says.

"What's that?"

"I know I want to see you again, as soon as possible!"

"Me too!" I gasp, my whole body turning to mush.

J D Baird © 2022

"I've never been this forward; I don't want to regret anything!" Ben declares.

"Are you sure about that?" I joke with him. "Too soon?"

"Too soon!" he responds, and we both laugh, hard.

"Daniel, you make me feel something I really can't explain, it's like my whole body wants to explode with happiness. I really don't know what you have done to me."

"You're breaking my heart!" I laugh, but I know I feel exactly the same way about him.

"I'd never break your heart," he fires back quickly.

"I'm really glad you called."

"I should hope so," he laughs. "I know how it feels, waiting for a guy to call. I didn't want to do that to you," he teases.

"I'm sorry!" I chuckle.

"But are you?" we both laugh again.

"I am, Ben. I am sorry," I try to say with an air of seriousness but he's having none of it.

"Well, you are forgiven."

"Why, thank you!" I respond, laughing.

J D Baird © 2022

We talk for such a long time, and it is by far the best conversation I have had in my entire life. I long to be with him, to hold him, to touch him, to kiss him. We say our goodnights and arrange to meet tomorrow. *'Tomorrow can't come soon enough'* I think to myself as I undress and climb into bed. I feel so happy, so alive.

***

I sleep for a couple of hours before being awoken by Stella, rattling her keys in the door. I hear a few stumbles and a leg bang on the coffee table, followed by a howl. I hear drunken footsteps heading towards the bathroom. There's more clambering around before I hear the toilet flush and the squeak of the tap being turned on, then off again. My door creaks open slowly, I open one eye, try to focus on the door and Stella's head creeps in.

"Goodnight," she whispers and blows me a kiss, stumbling backwards.

"Goodnight," I whisper back, returning the kiss.

I hear Stella climb into bed; she's probably fully dressed but that's normal for her. Moments later, I hear snoring. I smile to myself, turn over and close my eyes.

CHAPTER 7 - ICE CREAM AND DOGS

I wake up and check my phone, **'Good morning! x'** this instantly puts the biggest grin on my face. **'Good morning! x'** I reply. I get out of bed and hop into the shower. On the way back to my room, I check in on Stella, as predicted, she is fully clothed. She is the wrong way up in bed and her eyes are a lovely shade of black mascara.

"Good night?" I ask her.

She groans and rolls over. I walk back to my room, sit on the bed and notice there's another text from Ben asking about today. I reply and we agree to meet at the same place we went for coffee yesterday, at around 11am.

I have butterflies in my stomach as I worry about what to wear. I never worry about clothes, they are just a simple necessity, but somehow a date with Ben has me in a spin and I seem to have lost the power of rational thinking. I want to make a good impression but not too much, so I settle on long denim shorts and a white t-shirt, I put on fresh white socks and my black Vans.

I go into the kitchen and pour out some cornflakes into the only clean bowl I can find, and I wash up a spoon. After opening the fridge and finding out there isn't any milk, I eat them dry and pour myself a large glass of orange juice. I look at the clock, it's 10.07am, so I grab my phone, wallet and keys and shove them into my pockets, I call out to Stella and let her know I'm leaving. She responds with another groan.

"I'll call you later!" I tell her and leave the flat.

It's a nice walk to the coffee house, the warm sun is shining down on my face and as I walk through the park, I hear children shouting and dog's barking, it is merry, and the air is full of life. Children are running up and down and some are whizzing around on bikes, I had to dodge one small child on a red bike without pedals. He wore a yellow helmet, and his knees and elbows were padded. Dogs are chasing sticks and taking them back to their delighted owners who throw them as far as they can, and the process is repeated. There's a group of young boys playing football on the green and they are calling out to each other to 'pass.' My heart feels as happy as the atmosphere around me, it feels almost like this day was made for me.

As I walk towards my destination, I see him. He's sat outside, scrolling through his phone, air pods in his ears. He's wearing an oversized black t-shirt and black shorts. His eyes are covered by sunglasses and his hair is tied back. He looks like he is in a good mood, I take a moment to capture his beauty and my heart skips a beat. I take a huge breath before stepping closer, he has noticed me.

"Hi!" he says standing up, removing his earphones and shoving his phone in his pocket.

"Hi!" I reply.

There's an awkward moment between us, should we shake hands? Hug? Kiss?

"Coffee, one sugar?" he remembers, breaking the ice.

"Yes please!" I say politely, sitting down as he disappears inside.

J D Baird © 2022

I take out my phone and text Stella, but receive no reply, she is likely to be still in the same position as I left her. I lock my phone and put it into my pocket. Ben appears and sits opposite me.

"So how are you?" he asks with a huge smile.

"I'm great!" I reply. "How about you?"

"I'm good!" he says, still smiling. "I hardly slept last night," he continues. "I couldn't stop thinking about you."

I feel my stomach tensing and the smile on my face confirms to him that I feel the same.

"Me too!" I say. "Stella went out last night and I have left her in a booze induced coma."

"Will she be ok?" he asks, concerned.

"Oh yea, absolutely," I respond. "This isn't the first time and won't be the last!" I laugh.

The coffee arrives and we talk more about trivial topics. He doesn't mention Eric, thank goodness. I really didn't want to hear any more about him. The thought of him and Eric repulses me. Eric seems just so… strange. I can't quite put my finger on it but the less he is topic of conversation the better.

J D Baird © 2022

"So, what shall we do today?" Ben asks.

I really haven't thought this far, just seeing him was enough for me.

"I'm not sure!" I respond. "Do you fancy anything?"

"You!" he says and takes my hand.

I can feel the heat rising in my inner core and I can do nothing else but smile at him.

"Maybe we should take a walk through the park?" I suggest, whilst trying to regulate my body temperature, which is immensely hard considering it is, again, one of the hottest days of the year.

"Yea, sure!" he agrees. "That sounds good.

We walk to the park and find a good spot to sit, it's in front of the pond, and an ideal place to people watch, always a good topic of conversation. On the other side of the pond is an ice-cream van with a queue of sweaty children and impatient parents. We watch as a small girl drops her ice-cream, and a seagull instantly picks it up and flies away with it. There's a couple sat not too far from us with a picnic and blanket, they look madly in love, feeding each other strawberries, laughing and embracing. I look at Ben.

"Have you ever been in love?" I ask him, not knowing why I would ask such a question.

"I once loved a girl," he responds to my surprise.

"Go on," I probe.

"Well, it was a long time ago, back in school. I was around fourteen or fifteen. Long story short, she broke my heart."

"Ok," I say, intrigued. "What happened?"

"It was the end of year disco, and she turned up with another boy. We had been dating for about 6 months."

I laugh. I really don't mean to and Ben glares at me.

"Sorry!" I say, still laughing.

"It's not funny!" he says back, trying not to laugh.

"Oh, but it is!" I tell him and he pushes me, so I push him back.

"Have you ever been in love?" he returns the question.

I think about it for a second, "No!" I respond.

J D Baird © 2022

He looks deep into my eyes, trying to read my thoughts. The pain of losing my mum had put a barrier around my heart, I was scared to love, and the way Ben makes me feel terrifies me.

"Ice-cream?" he asks.

"Yea sure!" I say and we stand up and stroll over to join the queue.

There is a lady in front of us, holding a chubby, already sticky toddler in her arms, who is facing us, and he pokes out his tongue. Ben does it back before almost being caught by the woman.

"Stop!" I tell him as I reach over and grab his hand.

It was intended to be his arm. My hand stays where it is. He looks down, and studies my actions before intertwining his fingers into mine. The feeling is electric. I don't ever want this line to end, I could stay here, in this moment forever. The touch of his hand in mine was a feeling like no other. Could I possibly be falling? So soon?' Is this what it feels like? We reach the front of the line, and he lets go of my hand as he orders a large vanilla cone with a flake, I order the same and I pay.

J D Baird © 2022

We walk around the pond whilst discussing how delicious our ice-creams are, Ben bites a bit of his chocolate flake and I take mine out and eat it. They taste so good on this hot day. Ben takes a chunk of the cold, creamy whip on the end of his finger. I thought he was going to lick it off but instead, without warning, he plants it right on my nose. I scoop up a chunk from my ice-cream and wipe it on his cheek in retaliation.

"Hey!" he says playfully, wiping his cheek with the back of his hand.

"Hey you, first!" I reply.

He looks at me and opens his mouth like he's about to say something back but instead he comes closer and wipes the ice-cream from my nose with the gentlest touch and smears it softly on to my lips. His touch makes my heart begin to beat faster. He places a hand firmly on my lower back and he moves his face closer to me, I close my eyes and feel his lips brush mine, just as he is about to kiss me, a dog bounds over, steals the ice-cream from my hand and runs off. I open my eyes and Ben is laughing. A man shouts after his dog and apologises profoundly, he is clearly embarrassed. I lick the ice-cream from my own lips in disappointment.

"Come on!" says Ben, grabbing my hand again and pulls me along. "Want to share mine?" he asks, still laughing.

"No thanks!" I say smiling, but dejected, as we walk hand in hand.

I watch in silence as he finishes his ice-cream. *Is it possible to be jealous of ice-cream?* I think to myself. *Yes, it absolutely is!*

***

We leave the park and wander through the high street, looking in shop windows and discussing the items on display.

"Ben?" I ask out of the blue. "Were you serious about London and us staying together?"

He stands still and looks at me.

"Yes, of course I was!" he confirms. "Are you having second thoughts? It's ok if you are."

"No, not at all," I say. "I just wanted to make sure."

"So, let's do it now!" he says with impulse.

"Do what?" I ask confused.

"Let's find somewhere to rent."

We go to the estate agents and look around. Everything is happening so quickly, but it feels right. We find an apartment, within walking distance of the studio and settle on that. Rehearsals were going to take place in the studio, a short drive from the theatre, so everything was fairly close.

As we come out of the estate agents, with a deposit put down on the apartment and a firm guarantee we would have somewhere to stay, I feel overjoyed. It begins to rain, it is refreshing, and it feels nice on my skin, the hot air begins to cool. We walk a short distance along the street before Ben stops suddenly, he turns to me.

"I've always wanted to do this," he says.

"Do what?" I ask, looking up at him.

I watch as the rain drips down his face and a couple of loose strands of hair start to curl around his forehead. He pushes them back with the palm of his hand.

"This!" he whispers, pulling me close.

J D Baird © 2022

Without warning, he kisses me! Here, in the pouring rain. He kisses me, he puts his lips against mine, taking my breath away, everything I'd ever dreamt of, I felt like the world could end at any moment and I would still be the happiest man alive. I open my eyes and he looks down at my lips, I kiss him straight back, this time I wasn't going to let anything stop us. He holds my face as we kiss harder. The butterflies in my stomach had been released and are fluttering around in a frenzy.

"Third time lucky hey?" he says as he moves away.

I laugh as I pull him back and kiss him again. Nothing on earth could beat this feeling.

***

When I arrive back at the flat, Stella is awake and sat watching tv, she is curled up in a ball.

"Hey!"

"Hey!" she responds.

I sit down, next to her.

"You really need to shower!" I say.

"And you really need to tell me about your day!" she smirks. "And why on earth are you dripping wet?"

"It rained," I smile.

"Well?" she asks.

"I'll tell you later," I say getting up and walking away. "I have something important to tell you, but I need to change first."

"Daniel!" she screams and throws a cushion in my direction; it hits my back as I leave the room, the soft square inflicts no pain and she doesn't have the energy to get up and chase me, so I laugh at her.

I walk into my room, close the door, collapse onto my bed and read my messages.

"*Can't wait until next time x*"

"*Me neither x*" I reply.

'Could I be the happiest man alive?'

CHAPTER 8 – HE COOKS?

I had spent the last few days hanging out with Ben after work, if we weren't physically in each other's company, we were talking on the phone. We leave for London in two days, and I have been lucky enough to get the time off work, unpaid of course but fortunately mum's inheritance has really helped with my short-term financial situation.

Stella still can't believe I will be living with him but she's totally crazy herself and keeps telling me she would have done the same.

"Are you sure this is the right thing to do?" she asks me for the forty - fifth time this morning. "I mean, I would of course, you know me, but Daniel, this is you."

She will not put any doubt in my mind, it's made up.

"Stella, we've gone through this, I am moving there anyway, plus I've never been happier, you know how I feel about him."

"How do you feel about him?" she asks me cautiously.

"Got to go!" I say heading for the door. "I'm running late for work!"

I grab my keys off the table and leave before she has a chance to interrogate me further.

***

I make the 08.13 train on time and find a seat, it's a thirty-minute commute to the office, which is usually dull and uninspiring. I sit down and place my coffee cup on the table and rest my head back on the seat. My phone rings.

"Good morning!" I say with a grin.

I can't help it; my face naturally lights up at the sound of his voice.

"Good morning, beautiful!" responds Ben.

He's called every morning since the day we shared our first kiss. It's become a habit and I look forward to hearing his deep silky tones every day.

"How's the train today?" he asks.

"Same as always!" I say with a sigh, looking out of the window. "But obviously, much better when I'm talking to you."

"I was thinking..." he says.

"Yes?"

"Do you want to come over to my place later?" he pauses and waits for a response which I don't give him. "I'll cook!" he adds quickly.

"Can you cook?" I ask, not really knowing why this surprises me but still thinking about the initial question.

"Well come over tonight and find out," he teases. "I can meet you straight after work if that's good for you?" he suggests.

After thinking about it for a moment, I agree, and we talk a little more before saying goodbye for the day. I hate the goodbye part.

***

I stroll into the office and find work is as boring as ever. Today goes by slower than usual and I find myself watching the clock and staring out of the window at the streets below. I watch as people walk by, and I wonder where they might be going or what they might be doing for the day.

My thoughts are filled with images of Ben and the taste of his lips on mine. Although I'm hesitant, I really can't wait to see him tonight, but I feel slightly apprehensive at the thought of us being completely alone. Ben had mentioned that Drake was visiting his brother, Sid was out with Chloe, and he had the place to himself. I know I am more than comfortable spending time with him, and I can be myself in his company, but we have never actually been completely alone. Whenever we have been together there has always been people around, whether it be in the park, the coffee house or the museum. I've never kissed anyone in a museum, let alone in public, but when I'm with Ben, I feel free. I don't care about the bigoted views of the world anymore; I don't care about the staring or the tutting. Or even the 'disgust', I get lost in the moment every time I'm with him and I don't care who knows. I wonder what my dad would think if he could see me now.

***

J D Baird © 2022

Work is finally over, and I sign out. As I leave the building, I look up and just cannot believe my eyes, standing across the road is Ben, he is the most delightful sight to behold. His hair is tied up and covered with a large rimmed black hat, he's wearing grey checked trousers and a white shirt which is unbuttoned to his chest. He has his sleeves rolled up, his tattoos, which are artistically printed are visible. He is wearing braces over his shirt, his look is completed with chunky, black ankle boots. My gosh he is so fit! Mysteriously, he has one hand behind his back. I smile and walk over.

"I didn't expect to see you here babe!" I say, still grinning, stupidly.

He kisses me gently on the cheek as he produces a single red rose from behind his back.

"I wanted to surprise you!" he says sweetly, handing me the rose.

"You did! I expected to meet you at the station the other end," I say.

J D Baird © 2022

I trace my finger around the soft, red petals and take in the sweet scent of the flower.

"This is beautiful, thank you!"

"I didn't want to miss a single moment of you!" he says as he takes my hand. "Shall we?" he nods his head in the direction of the station.

"We shall!" I answer and we take a walk to the station.

The train ride back to Sheffield seems to disappear in a heartbeat. We sit and talk, laugh (a lot) and kiss.

"So, what are you cooking tonight? I asked suspiciously, scrunching up my eyebrows and narrowing my eyes at him.

"That's a surprise too," he says reaching across for my hand. "I thought we could stop and pick up a bottle of wine first?"

"Sounds like a good idea."

I look down at my rose and wonder if this is all a dream, if it is I know I never want to wake up. I speculate if anyone has ever felt this good before, right now that seems completely impossible.

The train comes to a halt, and we get off, the next time I step off a train with him will be in London, I think to myself. We leave the train station and hunt down the wine cellar which we find on Vale Street.

It's a quaint old shop, been here for over a hundred years or so we're told, by the very talkative owner. There are large wooden barrels inside where you can bring a bottle and refill, the walls are stacked high with countless varieties from around the world. After a lot of deliberation, and some indecision, we settle on two bottles of red wine from Italy.

The walk to Ben's house takes around fifteen minutes, it's a nice walk, the day is still fresh, and the sun is hot. The sky is bright blue and clear, I look up and see a flock of birds fly by. We reach a rather humble house. Surrounding the small, neat green garden is a pale grey, stone wall which has been divided by a small brown gate.

"This is me!" announces Ben and he opens the gate ushering me in.

We walk up to the archway in which a grey panelled front door sits. I watch as Ben takes his keys from his back pocket and unlocks the door.

J D Baird © 2022

"After you," he says, letting me in first.

I walk into the hallway with a knot in my stomach, I truly do still feel the same pang in my heart and excitement through my veins that I felt the moment I first ever laid eyes on him. He drops his keys into a bowl on a side table just inside the door and closes it behind him. He leads us in through to an open plan kitchen where a large table is laid for two.

"Ben this is great!" I say, utterly stunned that he would go to this much effort for me.

"Oh, it's nothing," he lies.

He walks over to a drawer and puts one of the bottles on the counter above, he roots inside the drawer and pulls out a corkscrew.

"Ah ha!" he says, still holding one of the bottles. "Grab some glasses!" he instructs, pointing to a cupboard door.

I open it and take out two glasses. He pops the cork on the bottle, and it instantly fizzes to the top.

"Shit!" he says as he runs to the sink and dangles the bottle over it.

I go and help him, taking the bottle from his hand and I pour the wine.

"Thanks!" he says, gratefully.

He turns around and switches on the oven..

"Is it always this organised here?" I ask, looking around and thinking back to the chaotic flat I share with Stella.

Shit, Stella! I quickly take out my phone and send her a text to let her know where I am. No doubt, she would be worrying by now as I'm always home.

"We have a cleaner," admits Ben. "There are four guys who live here, we really wouldn't cope without her!"

"Ahh, that figures," I say, sliding my phone back into my pocket.

"Shall we go and sit in the garden? It's a lovely night!" asks Ben and I agree.

We go out and sit on a patioed area, it reminds me of the night at The Duke as I look over at him, glass in his hand and he is just as handsome as then. If not more.

J D Baird © 2022

"Did it take long to remove that ridiculous tash?" he asks me.

He must have been thinking about that night too.

"Ha-ha! Yes, it did, it took a lot of scrubbing," I respond, feeling around under my nose.

"You know Daniel, you really did take my breath away that night," he says with a sigh, looking into my eyes. "I wasn't expecting to see you again after the audition but I'm so glad you chose to go to The Duke, even with the tash," he chuckles, as he leans forward and kisses me.

"You take my breath away every night," I say as the kiss is reciprocated.

He puts his hand on the back of my neck and pulls me closer, his touch is warm and strong. I place my hands at the bottom of his waist, and as the kiss intensifies as my hands move upwards slowly, the kiss is powerful which makes me weak with desire and I never want it to end.

J D Baird © 2022

The sound of the oven beeping breaks the kiss as Ben pulls away. I sigh heavily as he stands up. I adjust my trousers slightly as I stand up after him.

"Dinner's up!" he says, and we head inside.

I sit at the table which he has prepared and eagerly await what I'm about to be served.

"It smells amazing!" I call over to him, playing with a cotton napkin.

"Thank you!" he says, heading over with a glass oven dish, on his hands are large navy-blue oven gloves and this makes me chuckle to myself.

"Sweet and Sour Chicken," he declares proudly, as he puts the large dish in the middle of the table.

I look at it in delight as he heads back to the kitchen to get the rice and salad bowls.

"Tuck in!" he says, and I do.

I scoop up a serving and put it on my plate.

"Mmmmm, this tastes amazing Ben," I say after my first mouthful. "You are yet to disappoint me," I tell him.

J D Baird © 2022

"Thank you!" he says back.

He looks just as surprised at how good it tastes.

We talk about the night at The Duke as we eat, we both purposely don't talk about the night beyond the pub, we discuss Chloe and Sid, and we laugh at the state Drake had arrived in. I ask how he met his housemates, and he informs me that he went to college with Sid and Drake, but Eric arrived later, after somebody else gave up the tenancy. They didn't know him beforehand, but they got on very well with him and he fit in the friendship group well. This was the first time we had spoken about Eric since that night, other than Ben briefly explaining their night together. I shudder as I think about it. I don't know why but I ask him how Eric is.

"He's ok," Ben says and tells me he's been in contact with him over text recently. "He's recovering well at his parent's place, and he's told me he's sorry and swears he had just drunk far too much."

Ben admits he doesn't fully believe him, and he has yet to see it for himself.

J D Baird © 2022

"You see, after we slept together, he was very full on," Ben continues without me asking for more information. "I tried to tell him I wasn't interested in a relationship with him, but I didn't think he would take it that far."

I can see the sadness in Ben's eyes, and we continue eating in silence.

"There's ice-cream for afters," Ben spurts out suddenly and we laugh.

"Now you know how messy you can get with ice-cream!" I tell him.

"You too!" he smirks at me.

We head into the lounge to listen to some music and relax.

"It's been a long day!" I tell him, sitting back and putting my feet up on the coffee table.

"It sure has!" mutters Ben as he heads back into the kitchen to fetch the rest of the wine.

When he leaves I suddenly feel nervous, not the stage fright nerves that I've experienced many times before now. It's the type where I need to remember to breathe, and probably drink some more wine. He comes back in and joins me, putting his feet up and pouring me another glass. A song comes on the playlist.

"Do you remember this one?" he asks. "I love this song!" he says with excitement.

"I do! I admit and he starts to sing.

He's definitely not shy, or nervous around me. We talk some more about the songs playing and reminisce about our school days. We swap stories and enjoy being in each other's company. Having fretted about being alone with him, I start to feel totally at ease in his company. In fact, too comfortable.

"Take out your hair!" I request.

"Why?" he asks me.

I tell him just how hot it makes him look and I think the way I feel is written across my face. I watch as he slides out his hair band and runs a hand through his waves, I take his hand away from his hair and pull him closer, I can't resist him. I kiss him passionately and he leans his head back on to the couch.

I pull away from him and look into his eyes. He is beautiful. He closes his eyes and takes a deep breath.

J D Baird © 2022

As he leans to one side, I kiss his neck, I start to run my fingers around the top of his shirt slowly, it is already unbuttoned half the way down. I begin to unbutton the rest and he opens his eyes. He looks down at my hand and stops me as he places his hand over mine and he looks back up at me.

"Are you sure?" he asks, and I give him his answer with a kiss.

I no longer want to talk. He stands up and picks up the bottle of wine in one hand and the empty glasses in the other.

"Follow me," he whispers as he leads me upstairs.

J D Baird © 2022

CHAPTER 9 – SWEET SURPRISES

I'd spent the most incredible few days with Daniel, I've never been so happy in another person's company. Yesterday, we went to the museum, and I couldn't keep my hands off him. He looked amazing and tasted even better. He was stood in front of a description about an old car and was reading it. I crept up behind him and put my hands around his waist. A man walked past and tutted in our direction, we laughed. I didn't care anymore, I was falling for him, hard and I didn't care who knew. He turned around and kissed me.

"Not in here!" said a security guard, walking passed.

We laughed again and moved on.

***

I always knew I was gay from around the age of nine, I found boys far more attractive than girls, but I didn't really know why. I had girlfriends in school and just assumed I would marry a girl when I grew up as that was the right thing to do. Or so I was told. I didn't know anyone else like me. I was sixteen when I told my mum, she had always known, she told me. She embraced me and we both went and spoke to my dad. This was the hardest thing I had ever done; I was sure he was going to disown me, hate me, tell me it was wrong. He didn't.

"I love you, Ben!" he had said. "No matter who you are, or what you do, you will always make me proud."

I was one of the lucky ones I guess, my parents were accepting, and this gave me the confidence to live my life how I chose. They have always been by my side during every step I have taken.

***

Daniel is working today, so I call his phone, he should be on the train there now. He answers and my heart beats faster at the sound of his voice. I ask if he would like to come over tonight and he agrees.

I get dressed and head into the high street to pick up groceries for dinner, I should have asked him what he liked, but stupid me told him I'd surprise him. I walk around the supermarket in a panic, I have no idea what to cook really. I buy some chicken, a jar of sweet and sour sauce, an onion, rice and I pick up a bag of ready-made salad. On the way back, I head into the florist and buy a single red rose.

"She must be one lucky lady," said the older woman from behind the counter.

"I am the lucky one," I say as I hand over the money. "And for the record, 'she' is a 'he'," I correct her as she flushes a dark shade of pink.

"Thank you!" I say and I smile as I leave.

I get home and the cleaner is already there, she is just unplugging the vacuum cleaner.

"It looks amazing, Sophie. Thank you!"

"It's what you pay me for," she replies.

"Sophie?" I question. "Please could you stay and help me with the cooking?"

"Of course!" she says wrapping up the lead of the vacuum and moving it aside.

"Oh, and Sophie," I add. "Leave the table, I want to do that myself."

Sophie helps me prepare the chicken as I chop the onion, I take a couple of carrots from the fridge as instructed by Sophie, she suggests they will go well with it. Sophie shows me how to cook the rice and I empty the salad into a bowl, cover it and put it in the refrigerator. Sophie gives me instructions on when to pour the sauce over the chicken and how long to set the timer for before she leaves. I wonder if I'm making too much fuss, will Daniel be impressed? My head is in a spin, and I feel flustered.

I sit down and open a chilled beer; it's only midday and I am already so nervous. I plan surprising him outside his work later, but I can't help but wonder if this is the right thing to do.

Lately, I have found I question all my decisions where Daniel is involved. My heart seems to ache each minute I'm not with him, maybe I should text him. I take out my phone to text him and there's a message from Eric.

'Hi Ben, how are you? I feel so much better, the wound is healing nicely. Mum and dad tell me it's going to be a while before I should come home. The doctors say I have depression.

Not true, I was just drunk and stupid. Can't wait to see you again. I miss you!'

I feel sick. I really worry about him but at the same time he scares me. I need to talk to the others about him living here with us and whether it's a good idea that he returns. I really don't think I can share the house with him anymore. It's not right.

I reply:

'Hi Eric, glad to hear from you. It's great to know you are feeling better. Maybe take your parent's advice and stay there until you are fully fit.'

He replies instantly:

'Do you miss me too?'

'Yea of course we miss you'

I lie as I text back.

'Me, Sid and Drake all want you to get better but only come home when you are ready.'

'You will take care of me, won't you?'

I dodge the question.

'We all will.'

J D Baird © 2022

I don't want him to know how I really feel, he didn't take that too well the last time I was honest.

I finish drinking my beer and try to distract myself from thoughts of Eric returning. I totally forget to message Daniel and instead I go upstairs to shower and change. I pick out an outfit and grab my favourite black hat from my closet. I tie my hair up and pull out my braces from my top drawer, attaching them. They go great with these trousers; I think to myself looking in the mirror. I roll up my sleeves and slip on my watch. I pick up my ring and place it on my thumb. *'Ready as I'll ever be!'* I tell myself with one last check in the mirror.

***

I know Daniel finishes at 4pm so I decide to catch the 15.23 train to his office. I sit uneasily on the train, and stare at the rose in my hand. I feel a knot tighten in my stomach and it's not a nice feeling. I keep picturing Eric and replay the conversation in my head. The thought of him nauseates me, but he is a kind person and I'm sure he means no harm. *'He will get over it.'* I convince myself. I look out of the window and watch as the trees blur into a haze of green. I picture Daniel, our first kiss, I recall the way he makes me feel and my disgust slowly turns to delight.

***

The train pulls into the station, and I get off, I can't wait to see him. I straighten myself out and head over to where Daniel works, I arrive just in time to be there when he comes out. I wait across the road, and I hide the rose behind my back. I see him come out of the rotating doors of his office block and he spots me. He walks straight over. He is a sight to remember, white shirt and navy cropped trousers, he's wearing brown shoes and he looks so professional. A complete contrast to his dance wear or his 70's gear for that matter. *'He would look good in anything.'* I think to myself. He is very surprised to see me and after all my second guessing, I'm glad I made the decision to surprise him.

We catch the train back and the return journey seems so much shorter. Just being in his company fills me with warmth. He has the most beautiful smile, and I just can't take my eyes off him. We pick up two bottles of wine on the way back to mine.

J D Baird © 2022

When we arrive at the house, I take Daniel into the garden whilst the food cooks, we talk about the night we first met and I kiss him, I just can't help it, he's so darn irresistible. He puts both his hands on my waist, and I feel the strong grip of his hands intensify through my whole body, which deepens the kiss. We are interrupted by the ping of the oven telling me the food is ready. I've never been as nervous as I feel right now. I jump up and we head inside. Daniel sits at the table which took me fucking ages to lay and I laugh at myself, but he is clearly impressed. I bring the food over and we eat.

After dinner, we head into the lounge and I put on some music, I can feel my heart beating fast, so I get up and fetch the wine and the glasses from the kitchen. I come back into the lounge, and he is sitting on the couch with his feet on the table. I join him. Just sitting next to him relaxes my nerves, I feel completely at ease now. We talk about our old school days and how the songs remind us of certain situations. One of my favourite songs starts to play and this excites me. I even surprise myself by singing along. I can't help but grin when I see the way his eyes light up when he recalls a memory. He is perfect!

The music stops and the air falls silent. I look at him and he looks back with intense brown eyes, he asks me to take my hair out, so I do, it makes me feel slightly self-conscious, so I run a hand through my hair to straighten it out, the problem with curly hair is that it always looks like you've just woken up. He takes my hand away from my head and pulls me closer to him, he looks down at my lips, and kisses me. It feels so good, too good. I lay my head back onto the couch and as I close my eyes I feel the warmth of his lips on my neck. I bite my bottom lip in pleasure, I feel his hand against my chest, and he begins to unbutton my shirt. I look down and stop him.

"Daniel, are you sure about this?" I ask him.

He kisses me harder which gives me the answer I was hoping for. We head upstairs, wine bottle and glasses too.

I place the drink and glasses onto the side and take my phone out of my pocket. I switch it off. He watches me, he comes over to where I am standing, and he slips off each of my braces in turn and unbuttons the rest of my shirt and takes it off. I can't speak, I don't have to. I push him on to the bed and kiss him. His eyes tell me he's hungry for more and he sits up to face me. Still unable to speak, I unbutton his shirt and push it away from his shoulders, his bare skin invites me to kiss it, he lifts my head to face him, and I can't help but fall deeper and deeper into his spell. He is all I have ever wanted; all I have ever dreamt about. I hold his face and kiss him again; he runs his hands through my hair and down my back. The feeling is like no other, the touch of his hands on my body makes me groan with pleasure. He gently bites my bottom lip, and I feel my eyes roll to the back of my head. I've never wanted anything as much as I want him now. We fall onto the bed together...

J D Baird © 2022

CHAPTER 10 – LOOSE ENDS

I wake up with the sun in my eyes, still sleepy and I can hear Daniel in the bathroom. I squint and rub my eyes before stretching out my arms and yawning, loudly.

"Good morning, sleepy head," he says as he walks in and climbs back into my bed.

"Good morning, beautiful!" I say unable to take the smile off my face.

My gaze follows the shape of his face before resting on his lips.

"How are you?" he asks, pushing a wayward curl away from my eyes.

"I'm good," I say, not wanting to get out of bed so I pull him close to me.

His warm body melts into mine and I wrap my arms and legs around him.

"You know I have to go to work this morning," he tells me as I hold onto him tighter.

"I'm serious!" he says. "They are giving me the time off for London, so I have to be on my best behaviour."

I reluctantly unwrap my hungry limbs from him and flop back onto my pillow with a groan. I watch as he dresses, his lean, smooth body makes me tingle under the sheets. I lazily reach out to the side of the bed he slept in and stretch my arms even further trying to reach him and he laughs. He comes back over to me, kisses me on the forehead, and tells me he will call me later. This wasn't sufficient, he's left me wanting him again. I close my eyes and sigh at my sudden loneliness, snoozing a while before finally getting out of bed.

I head downstairs to make coffee. I look around and see the mess left from last night, so I open the dishwasher and begin to fill it, as I walk over to the kettle I see a note on the side:

"*You are incredible!*" it reads. My heart flutters.

Today is our last day in Sheffield and the thought of arriving in London with Daniel tomorrow excites me. I make coffee and sit in the lounge, replaying every moment of last night.

J D Baird © 2022

The clock turns 8.20am, he will be on the train to work now, so I call him.

"Hey, you!" he answers.

"You are too," I say, referring to the note he left me earlier.

"Thank you, I wasn't sure you would be up so soon." he says.

"I wouldn't miss our early morning chats for the world," I tell him, meaning every bit of it. I don't think he really knows just how much he means to me or just how intoxicating he is.

"Last day in Sheff today," he tells me.

"I know, we need to get the keys from the estate agents today. I can go whilst you're in work if you want," I inform him, "I've got a few things I need to tie up with work first and then I'll head in and get them.

"Yes, ok, are you packed yet?" he asks

"Almost," I tell him, my mind resorts to my half-packed bag in my room.

"Me too," he responds.

"Daniel, we really are doing this, together," I interrupt.

"Yes, we are, and I couldn't be any happier!" I hear the elation in his voice. "You really are incredible!" he adds.

I slump back into my seat, desperate to see him later.

I make more coffee and log into my laptop, check my emails and make a few calls to clients. It's important to let them know I'm going to be away for a few weeks, but their business is in good hands with my partners. I make sure I pay outstanding orders and send out a quote to the Jefferson's who we have worked with before, they are an extremely important client.

***

My dad ran a successful landscaping business before he retired. Dad started off as a gardener and odd job man before building up the family business, which he then proudly handed over to me two years ago. I started working for him when I was eighteen and worked on site with experienced gardeners. Since taking the business over, working from home has given me the freedom to pursue my dream and continue to dance. Dad has said he will keep an eye out, but he also trusts my judgement in handing it over for a few weeks.

I complete my morning tasks and as I'm about to head to the estate agents, Sid walks in grinning like a cat.

"Good morning, buddy!" he says taking his shades off, his eyes wide and his smile wider.

"Good morning, to you too. How's Chloe? And how was last night?" I question.

"Great!" he says, "You?"

"*Incredible!*" I tell him with a colossal smile on my face. "I'm just going to collect the keys for our London place."

"Is that still happening?" he looks at me inquisitively.

"Yes!"

"Amazing Ben, I'm really happy for you! You know where we are if you need me or Drake, and please, whatever you do, don't think about Eric whilst you're gone. There's no need, he's safe with his parents and if he comes back, we will take care of him. I'm sure he will have figured out his feelings by the time you are back."

"Thank you!" I tell him and head out of the door with a spring in my step.

On the way to the high street, I daydream lightly, I recall his smell and the taste of his tongue, I can still feel the touch of his hands and I shiver. I look around and see people getting on with their day, but I can't help but feel like we are the only two people in the world. My phone vibrates in my pocket.

It's Eric. *'What the fuck does he want?'* I end the call, I really don't want to speak to him, or think about him. My phone vibrates again and it's a text,

'Hey Ben, I tried to get hold of you last night, but your phone was off, not to worry. I imagine you're busy now with work too. I'll try you again later. Miss you, Eric x'

I ignore it, shove my phone into my pocket and go and pick up the keys. I don't have time for his shit, I am really happy that he's getting better but I can't help but resent him, and the mistake I made. Sid's right, I need to ignore him.

When I get home, I continue to pack my belongings for London, I put on some motivational music and pack the entire contents of my dancewear. *'Should be enough'* I tell myself looking down at my bulging bag. I stretch the straps across the front and clip it securely.

Daniel calls a while later to ask me how it's all going; he's packing too and keeps checking in with me to see if we are making the right decision.

"It's too late now," I tell him.

I'm sure he is the one who has doubts, as there is absolutely no question in my mind. We are meeting later tonight for a drink with everyone to say goodbye. It's going to be odd leaving but it's only for a few weeks. This time last month, I was in a very different place, living with a group of guys, preparing for an audition that would change my life (at the time I just didn't realise how much it would change) and here I am now, about to set off on a new adventure and what better way to do it than to share it with a man who shares my dreams too.

CHAPTER 11 – SEE YOU TONIGHT

I get back from Ben's with a smile on my face, wider than the Pacific, the lingering aroma of him still on my body, I head straight to the shower, I need to leave pretty sharpish for my last day at the office. The warm water runs over my body, and I feel his warm hands all over again. I close my eyes, unable to shake the image of Ben from my mind and I don't want to. If this is what a dream feels like, I don't ever want to wake up. I try to focus on reality and get out of the shower, grab a coffee, get dressed and rush out to catch the train.

"See you tonight!" I call to Stella.

It's far too early, even if I had the time, to tell her about last night. I'd give anything right now to sit with her and tell her every pure detail, every perfect detail of last night.

I run for the train as it pulls into the station and find my seat, seven minutes into the journey and like clockwork, Ben calls. My heart pounds as I answer on the first ring, already holding my phone tightly in my hand, expecting his call. His deep voice falls into my ears, and I melt into the seat. He tells me about the estate agents and I'm pretty disappointed not to be going with him to pick up the keys, but I get to spend the next few weeks with him, just him and this fills me with happiness.

The train suddenly arrives at the platform, so we end our conversation, I almost kiss my phone before putting it back into my pocket.

The smile doesn't leave my face the entire time I'm at work and a few people in the office tease me. I get many well wishes and congratulations for London too. There are some genuinely nice people here and I consider myself lucky to work with them. There is of course the odd few who couldn't care less. My boss is really supportive however, I've been here for the last two years and never missed a day. The day drags but it is made bearable by the huge cake we share at lunch.

I literally sprint out the door at 4pm, and call Ben, I can tell by his voice, he is pleased to hear from me. He's packing.

When I arrive home, Stella is waiting.

J D Baird © 2022

"And where the fuck were you last night?" she laughs. "Don't tell me! No, you didn't, No way?" Tell me!" she says.

"You just said don't tell you," I tease.

"Jesus, tell me!" she says impatiently so I eagerly tell her everything.

Almost everything.

"Oh my gosh, Daniel, do you love him?" she asks.

"No, don't be silly!" I tell her, picturing his sleeping face, longing to curl back under the covers with him and desperately hold him close, his body intertwined with mine and the moonlight on my back but instead I had to part from him to get back to reality and complete my last shift before London.

"Daniel, I have never seen you like this before, and I know you. Do you love him?" she asks me again, studying the look in my eyes.

"I don't know," I say. "I mean, I feel all these kinds of feelings. I can't wait to see him; I can't wait to hold him. I miss him when he's gone. I feel like my world could come crashing down at any moment."

J D Baird © 2022

"Oh, wow! You do love him!" Stella informs me.

'*Maybe I do*' I think to myself as I get up to leave.

"We are meeting later, remember," I tell her.

"I know, you fool!" she says. "I wouldn't miss it for the world! Leaving drinks in The Duke."

"*The Duke!*" I repeat quietly.

I head into my room and look around, sighing to myself, pick up some dirty laundry from the floor and throw it towards the open door. I finish packing, well, I think I'm done. I look at my bag on the bed and imagine what it will be like living in London with Ben, I hardly know him. I start to doubt myself, so I call him again and ask him if we are making the right choice and he reassures me that we are. He tells me that he could not be happier. I believe him.

"I'll see you tonight!" I tell him.

"Can't come soon enough!" he says.

I almost forget about the real reason we are both going there, only a month ago, I didn't have this life. I didn't feel this free. So much can change in an instant.

J D Baird © 2022

CHAPTER 12 – GOODBYE AT THE DUKE

"Come on Daniel!" calls Stella from the living room.

"Cheers!" she says and hands me a beer.

"Cheers!" I reply and tap her bottle.

I look at her, wondering if she will be ok without me. Then I think about all the times she has looked after me, of course she will be fine.

"I'm really going to miss you," she tells me as her eyes well up. She lurches forwards and clasps her arms around me in the tightest embrace ever.

"I love you Daniel, you're my best friend."

"It's not forever." I tell her, trying to refill my lungs with air as she lets go slowly.

"I know," she says and hugs me again, this time with a little less strength. "Now let's go!"

    We get into an uber, and she looks at me with a heavy expression. She studies my face, looking for clues to the question she is about to ask.

"Will you tell him?"

"Tell him what?" *Is she talking about mum?* I wonder.

"That you love him, of course?" she blurts out.

"No way!" I assert. "Absolutely not, no way Stella, and you better not say a word tonight…because I don't!"

"I won't," she promises. "But you better call me, the instant you tell him."

"I will," I say without thinking…. realising I love him.

Oh! How my heart hurts, I love him!

***

We get to The Duke, and everyone is inside, Bernie, Drake, Sid and Chloe, I can't see Ben! For a second I worry he's not coming. He's at the bar. I puff the air out of my cheeks and gesture to Stella to go and sit with the others. I walk over to him and place my hands gently over his eyes.

"Daniel!" he says as he turns around opening his bright green eyes that say kiss me.

"Fancy meeting you here," I say.

It's an explosive moment, the place where we first really, truly met. I was desperate to pull him into me.

"I really want you!" he whispers in my ear.

"Me too," I reply, and we both look at our group of friends. "Later?"

"Later," he agrees passing me two drinks.

We take the cold glasses over to the table and I sit down with the others. Ben pulls a stool from a nearby table and sits down next to me, he puts his hand on my leg and grips it firmly before taking it off and picking up his pint. I look up to see Stella, eyeballing me, and I nearly choke on my drink. Ben looks straight at my face, concerned.

"Are you ok?" he asks putting a hand on my back.

"Yes," I splutter before glaring back at Stella.

We all sit and talk about what is going to happen in London.

"We will be rehearsing for two weeks and performing in the theatre for five nights, Monday to Friday," Ben informs the others.

J D Baird © 2022

They arrange amongst themselves to come and see our final show.

"Let's put on some music!" says Stella standing up and shuffling out of her space at the table, she heads to the jukebox, Bernie and Chloe get up and join her.

Ben and I head out for a smoke, I put a cigarette in my mouth and lift my lighter, Ben takes it out of my mouth and holds my hand encasing the lighter too, he kisses me.

"I've really missed you," he says, searching my eyes.

"Man, I've missed you too," I tell him kissing him back, wishing I could take him home, right now!

He stops and looks inside at our friends.

"Do you think they will miss us?" he asks.

"Probably not!" I say with a grin. "Probably looking forward to getting rid of us for a while."

We head back inside and sit back down; more drinks are ordered, and the girls return to their seats.

"How's Eric?" booms Bernie, loudly over the music and we all fall silent.

J D Baird © 2022

It's a deathly silence. I look down to my beer and can feel Ben looking at me, this time I don't look up. It's the first time I've felt uneasy around him. I can see him trying to say something and Stella puts her hand in mine.

"He's ok," blasts Sid quickly. "I called him yesterday."

"Did you?" asks Chloe, surprised.

"Yea, I forgot to say, anyway, he's absolutely fine."

I lift my drink to my mouth and take a swig.

"I'm sorry Daniel," whispers Ben, turning to face me.

"It's not your fault," I whisper back.

"Are you ok?"

"Yes, I'm fine," I say.

We spend another hour or so chatting and laughing before it's time at the bar.

"That's it!" shouts Bernie. "Time to go, drink up everyone."

We finish our drinks and head outside. The cool air hits my face as I look around at the people supporting Ben and I, the smiles and the well-wishing, I feel unbelievably fortunate to be blessed with such an amazing group. I feel confident leaving Stella behind with such great people.

Chloe and Bernie leave in an Uber after saying goodbye, they wish Ben and I luck and tell us to stay safe. Ben is leaving with Sid and Drake,

"I guess I'll see you in the morning?" he says, looking my way.

"You sure will!" I respond and I turn to leave.

"Fuck it!" he says, grabbing my shirt, pulling me back, he kisses me goodbye.

"Shit!" says Stella as we climb into our Uber. "Now that was some kiss!"

My head swirls and my lips tingle as though they could set alight at any moment.

"I know!" I say quietly.

I head into my room, still feeling slightly nervous about the morning, but excited too. I move my bag from my bed and lie down. I pick up my phone.

CHAPTER 13 – LONDON'S CALLING

I wake early the next morning, I hardly slept last night, unable to untangle the knot of anxiety in my stomach. I'm meeting Ben at the station at 9.30am, the train to London leaves at 10.15am and we want to make sure we have plenty of time.

I walk into Stella's room.

"Hey Stella!" I say softly. "I'm leaving soon."

She dives up out of her covers and springs across the bed.

"Nooo," she jokes with me, grasping my leg and tugging desperately.

"Coffee?" I ask her, pulling away from her inferior grip and clearing up the empty water bottles beside her bed.

"Yes! I'll be out in a sec," she says. So I proceed to the kitchen and make two coffees, I put extra sugar in Stella's because I know getting up this early will be a major shock to her system.

She walks in the room and sits down.

"Thank you," she says. "Can you grab me two paracetamol?" she asks. "My head is throbbing."

"That will be the copious amount of alcohol," I scorn her.

She groans.

"So, you really are doing this?" she calls over as I remove the tablets from a drawer and run the cold tap.

"Yes!" I say, sitting down with her, I hand her the tablets and the glass then I look over to my bag. "I really am."

"When do you leave?"

"In around 20 minutes," I say, looking up at the clock hanging on the wall.

We sit patiently and stillness fills the room, the only movement is the coffee cups to our lips and back down again. I look up at the clock once more.

"It's time," I say, replacing the hush and clogging the room with my words.

"I guess it is," Stella nods, tearfully and we both stand.

She wraps her arms around me and kisses my cheek.

"I really do love you Daniel."

"I love you too!" I say and kiss her gently on her soft forehead.

J D Baird © 2022

"Just you make sure he looks after you right!" she says, wiping away her tears, her face red with sadness. "Any problems and I'll be on the first train there; you know that don't you?" she voices an air of seriousness, but I can tell her head still hurts.

"I will be absolutely fine; I can look after myself!" I convince her.

We hug again and I pick up my bag.

"Take care Stella," I say and leave the flat.

I look around with a heavy heart and she's perched in the doorway. Football socks to her knees, checked green shorts and a huge grey t-shirt. Her hair is a ball of mess, tied loosely on top of her head. She blows me a kiss goodbye and I catch it, kiss my fist and put it in my pocket. I turn away and head down the stairwell.

***

Ben is standing outside the station when I arrive, he looks as good as ever. He's wearing skinny black jeans and a white t-shirt, but the chill in the morning air has him covered with a red and black checked shirt. He looks extremely handsome and he's waiting for me. The luckiest man in Sheffield.

J D Baird © 2022

"Hey you!" I say as I get closer.

"Hey!" he calls out, eagerly as he spots me, he picks up his rucksack and swings it onto his back. "You look great!" he says as he kisses me on the cheek.

I look down at my choice of outfit, cream fitted shorts and a light blue, long sleeve shirt, which I've folded up to my elbows and buttoned halfway.

"Thank you, you do too! I reply.

We make our way inside the station and find a small café to wait in, we have plenty of time before the train arrives. I study our bags at the side of the table, and he lifts up my hands, cupping them into his.

"I'm really glad we are doing this - together; you make me so happy," he grins at me.

His eyes, his smile, his hair, his voice they are all overwhelmingly intoxicating, and I feel myself drown in his words. Without realising, he has a knack, a special power, which takes away all my concerns in an instant.

J D Baird © 2022

We order coffee and breakfast, I am feeling distinctively peckish, so I order an egg sandwich, Ben orders bacon. Afterwards, we head down to the platform and stand amidst the other travellers. I take his hand and he looks at me, his face looks more beautiful than ever, wide green eyes and the perfect jawline. I don't know how he became all mine but I'm never letting him go.

"Weirdos!" said a voice walking past us.

I look up and see two teenagers, dressed in baggy jeans and wearing caps, glaring back at us, both laughing. They put two fingers towards their mouths, gesturing the act of making themselves sick.

"Sickos!" one of them calls out, continuing to walk on, continuing to laugh.

I let go of Ben's hand at once.

"Ignore them!" he says, taking my hand back.

The train arrives and we get on, we haul our bags into the bagging area above our heads and take our seats. I sit by the window and look out, hurtful words still ringing in my ears. Ben climbs in next to me and smiles gently.

J D Baird © 2022

"It's going to be so much fun in London!" I exclaim, distracting myself from my thoughts.

"Daniel. We are going to be working hard too. We will have so much to do." he says with a serious tone.

"Yes, I know that! But isn't this what dreams are made of Ben?" I reply.

"It sure is!" he puts a hand in mine and tilts his head back. I face the window.

About an hour into the journey, I wake up with my head on Ben's shoulder and his head is resting against mine, his hair tickles my forehead. I shake him gently.

"Are we here?" he asks startled.

"No," I laugh. "I need to go to the toilet."

He shifts over and lets me out of my seat. When I return, I look down into the seat and his eyes are closed so I nudge him again.

"Ben!"

"Sorry," he says, and he moves to let me back into my seat. "I didn't sleep too well last night," he mumbles.

J D Baird © 2022

I wonder if he was having second thoughts. Of course not. It was his idea.

***

Eventually, the train arrives in London, and we take our bags down and exit. The platform is unpleasantly hot and extremely busy, Ben takes off his shirt and ties it around his waist, he pulls his large bag on his back.

"Let's get out of here!" he says, covering the glare from the sun with black shades.

I agree and haul my bag onto my shoulders.

We stand on the incredibly, packed London streets, surrounded by tourists and day trippers, we take in our new surroundings. It is such a contrast to the small village we share back up North. I take out my sunglasses and put them on to see better. The noise fills my ears almost instantly, making it difficult to hear, the ringing of impatient cyclists, the hum of cars, the traffic is whizzing by before my eyes. I see an open topped bus, full of people with cameras.

"We should do that," Ben says pointing to the top deck.

I stop and look at him, I find myself being physically drawn to him once more, I know it's hot out here, but he is the absolute definition of hot.

"So, it's not too far from here is it?" he asks, lighting up a cigarette.

I take out my phone to check the directions.

"No, it's close, we can jump on the tube or walk for 20 minutes?"

"Walk!" we both firmly agree.

It's 31 degrees today and London feels like hell.

CHAPTER 14 – MEETING THE CAST

We arrive at our apartment and go in through the main door, it's a buzzer entry system, not too complicated. There's a short staircase directly in front of us which leads up to the temporary front door of our home for the next three weeks, luckily, we only have the one flight, being on the first floor. Ben turns the key in the lock, and we go inside. I look around, my bag still on my back.

I'm pleasantly surprised at the vastness of the living area; it looks much bigger in person than the pictures back at the Sheffield estate agents. It's similar in layout to the flat I share with Stella; however, this place has a balcony area with patio style doors, adjacent to the kitchen. The kitchen area is in the corner, it's not huge but has everything we need, kettle, toaster, oven, microwave. A square dining table with four chairs takes up a portion of the living area, I turn around and see a huge blue couch with side tables and opposite, a decent sized television, although not wall mounted, it sits on a wooden stand in front of the white wall. There's a modest bathroom with shower and… then I see it, the bedroom. One bedroom. It just dawned on me that we will be sharing the room. In our haste to rent, I hadn't thought this far. I stop and stare into the room contemplating the velocity of my current situation.

"Is everything OK?" Ben asks me, appearing behind me and wrapping his arms around my waist.

"Yes," I say turning to him, the feel of him draped warmly around me reassures my mind.

He untwines himself and steps into the bedroom, he walks over to the large window and looks out. I join him and look onto the wide cobbled street. I feel at ease. We look over a fenced green. Ben moves away and sits on the bed, pushing down to feel the firmness with his hand. He looks up at me.

"Which side do you want?"

"I don't mind," I reply.

"Hmm, ok, I don't know about you, but I need a shower," he states, standing up to untie the shirt from his waist.

He pulls his t-shirt over his head, revealing his broad, bare chest, he moves in my direction and wraps his t-shirt around my waist.

"You're looking pretty hot too," he says kissing me with sweaty lips.

He leaves the room to shower, and I sit on the bed, flustered by the heat. I call Stella.

"Hey babe! Just calling to let you know we arrived!"

"Hey Dan! How was the journey?"

"Hot!"

"Ahh yea, it sure is. Well, enjoy every moment and call me again soon!"

"I will."

I hang up the phone and look in the mirror, Ben is right, I do need to shower, the dust from the London air is already in my hair and on my skin. Doesn't help that my skin feels as sticky as honey.

"Dan, we need to be at the studio by 4pm," Ben says as he comes back into the room with a towel tied around his waist.

I can't help but think about his gorgeous, defined body underneath, the water drips from his hair and he rubs it with another small, white towel. I gaze at him as his hair curls up even more with the moisture. He throws the towel on to the bed, and he walks back out of the room to hunt through his bag for a fresh t-shirt. He returns to the room and like a dog, he shakes his head as it appears through the gap, splashes of cool water land in my face.

"Oi!" I say, wiping my wet forehead and I head towards the shower, taking my bag in with me.

I shower and change in the bathroom and when I emerge, I notice he's fully dressed. He's sitting at the dining table, he's texting someone. I walk over to him and place my hands on his shoulders, I bend forward and kiss the back of his neck.

"Hey babe!" he says as he places his phone down on the table and turns his head towards mine.

I run my hand through his now dry hair, he smells incredible. My hand stops at the back of his head and he's looking up at me, he runs his tongue over his bottom lip and bites the edge, inviting me to kiss him.

J D Baird © 2022

"I'm so hungry!" he says, looking deep into my eyes.

"Me too," I tell him, and I kiss him.

Leaving the rest of the unpacking until later, we decide to head out for food and become familiar with our new city.

We find a small café and order sandwiches, which we decide to take out and eat on the go. We walk around for a while before making our way to the studio.

We arrive at a large warehouse which has been converted into dance studios, which is used by theatre companies and dance schools working in The West End. We step in together and I look around, the large space is full of dancers, choreographers and the production team. Amanda welcomes everyone in and congratulates us all once again. I look at Ben and he's smiling.

"So, let's meet you all," she says, thrilled and calls us up in turn.

"Ben Thomas, you will be playing Matthew," she smiles and gestures to him to join her.

He stands and looks down at me, for the first time I see his vulnerability. There's a roar of applause and whooping as he heads in Amanda's direction. I feel myself blush with pride. He's all mine, I think as I look at him, he graciously takes in the glory.

"And Daniel, you will be portraying the lovely Elijah."

I get up to the sound of clapping and stand by Ben. It's easier for me as he is already up there, I just have to stand by his side.

"Now, you two will be working *very* close to each other," she tells us. "So it's important that you take some time to get to know one another."

We look at each other and there's the sound of laughter, wolf whistling and another round of applause.

The rest of the cast list is called and one by one the performers join us. It's a feeling like no other. This is the first time we have seen each other as a group and the atmosphere is exciting. There's one last thrilling round of applause by everyone. As I clap, I look around and wonder just what I did to have all my dreams come true at once. We are given some time to talk to each other and break the ice. There are some vaguely, recognisable faces from the audition and some brand new. I look in Ben's direction, he's not really speaking to anyone, instead I see him take his phone from his pocket, look at it and put it straight away.

Amanda brings us all back together to run through some basic housekeeping rules, schedule for the rehearsals for the next two weeks and what to expect in the live shows. She then hands out scripts and informs us that we should all go away tonight and read them, so that we can discuss any concerns when we meet again tomorrow morning.

"So, that's it for today!" Ben says as Amanda wraps up. "It's going to be hard work from now on!"

We hang around for a while talking to some of the other dancers, we decided to keep our relationship quiet for the moment, just in case it has a negative impact on the rest of the cast.

Elated and full of joy, we head back to the apartment.

"So that was pretty interesting," I conclude as I sit down on the settee and Ben sits with me, script in his hand.

"Let's find the juicy parts then, Elijah!" Ben kids, as he flicks through.

J D Baird © 2022

We don't have many lines to say, but one in particular jumps right off the page and down my throat. I gulp.

"I love you!" I read in my head. "Matthew, I love you!"

Fear runs deep through my veins, as I think, not so long ago, my biggest problem was a kiss. Now *Elijah* must declare his love to *Matthew*.

We have a few drinks and talk about the other cast members before heading to bed. I decide to take the side closest to the window and Ben climbs in after me.

"This is perfect!" he whispers.

His phone vibrates on the table, and he ignores it. Instead, he turns to me and strokes a finger across my face and stops at my lips.

"Kiss me!" he demands.

***

I wake early the next morning, and I look across at a snoring mop of hair.

"Ben, wake up, rehearsals start at seven," I murmur as I stroke the smoothness of his back as he lies face down with one arm above the pillow. "Come on, lazy!" I say, kissing his back before climbing out of bed.

"Uggghhh!" he groans. "Completely your fault Dan," he says turning my way. "You kept me awake half the night."

When we arrive at the studio, we are greeted with smiles and nods. We are meeting with the choreographers to learn the new routines today and to my delight, I see a large silver urn full of coffee and all kinds of pastries laid out - we both could use the energy!

"Hi Daniel!" a voice calls out from behind us, Ben and I both turn to see a short man, heading our way.

"He looks rather excited," Ben whispers into my ear and chuckles.

"Ssshh!" I demand, holding in a laugh.

"How did you find the script?" the guy asks.

He's wearing a stripy blue and white t-shirt and holding a dancer's handbook in one hand and waving the script in the other. Ben raises his eyebrows at me and smiles. He nods politely to the new arrival then leaves and heads towards the refreshments.

J D Baird © 2022

"Hi Adam!" I say.

I met Adam last night, and he's somewhat eccentric. He takes a chair and gestures me to sit down too, before I've even taken my seat he's in my face, blabbing on, and on about his character and the changes he's hoping to make. He explains that a different perspective will give him an angle. I really don't know what he's talking about, he's a dancer, not a soap star. I look over in Ben's direction, he's been joined by an unfamiliar male. He laughs as they talk. The guy passes Ben the milk and continues to talk to him; the conversation between them looks far more interesting than my current one.

"OK everyone!" calls Amanda, loudly. "Let's gather round."

'Perfect timing!' I think to myself. Adam would have most probably told me the entire contents of his life story; had he not been interrupted. We're asked to sit in a large circle.

"Ben, Daniel? Where are you?" asks Amanda, scanning the room with her eyes, "Ahh there you are!" she spots us. "I told you yesterday, you will be very close on this one, so you may as well start by sitting together. From now on," she continues. "Unless instructed, I want to see you together, taking breaks together and really just getting to know each other."

'Now that won't be hard.' I think to myself and to my relief, Ben stands up and swaps seats with Adam.

"Sorry buddy!" says Ben sympathetically, faking a sad face.

"Hi Daniel!" he laughs, tapping me hard on the back as he sits down.

He smells like last night; I bite down on my lip to stop myself from biting him.

"Hi Ben!" I say, looking his way, as he slowly licks his lips.

My god, he can read my mind!

We are placed in groups to learn the dance routines and it's going really well. I realise I have never seen Ben dance before. His energy is amazing, his posture is graceful, he learns the steps quickly and I can see why he was chosen. He is everything they were looking for. He is everything I've ever wanted. We eventually get a break.

"Cigarette?" he asks me.

"Yes!" I say and we head out through the fire exit and onto the steps.

He pulls me in to him and kisses me gently, relieving the desperation my mouth has felt all morning. Mid-kiss, I hear footsteps behind me making me turn around. Adam!

"You take your roles seriously then?" he asks us both, suspiciously.

"Yes, of course. Just doing as instructed by Amanda," Ben says. "Don't you?"

"Absolutely!" he says, making himself appear taller by straightening out his back.

He joins us for a cigarette, and we smoke in silence.

"Coffee? I suggest, stamping out my cigarette along with the air of awkwardness and we all go back inside.

The afternoon consists of more practice, and it feels as though the first dance is coming together well. It is clear from

Adam's facial expressions that he has his suspicions about us, more than once this afternoon, Ben and I have caught him looking our way.

"He seems okay," I tell Ben on our walk back to the apartment.

"If you say so," Ben responds. "Personally, I find him a bit creepy, watching us all day. You know what, tomorrow we will give him something to really watch."

I laugh at Ben, wondering what we could possibly do to rouse his suspicions further.

CHAPTER 15 – I LOVE YOU

It's day three of rehearsals and it all still feels like a dream, my surroundings couldn't get any better than this, not to mention doing the job I love. It's a far cry from the office. This is what I was born to do, this is my calling, my whole body feels alive. I feel energised today and ready to take on the world, especially after waking up to the sound of the capital's bird song and the soothing rhythm of London's beating heart.

Today in the studio, we are rehearsing the 'kiss' scene between Matthew and Elijah, the script calls for a gentle, romantic first kiss between the two lovers.

The music starts and Ben and I begin to dance, he makes his way across the floor in time to the music, an arm falls onto my shoulder as I sweep underneath, lifting my face to his, a sudden turn and I bend towards the floor, he draws me to an upright position. The music is quick, the moves are quick. We stand back-to-back with individual steps, the choreography is tricky, and we have not danced together before, the music slows down and Ben pulls me around and into his body, I can feel his heart beating and his chest rising up and down. It matches the pattern of my own. There's a pause - He grabs my face and kisses me hard!

"Cut! Cut!" cries Amanda but Ben continues to kiss me.

"Enough!" Amanda demands loudly and he stops, the pair of us look at her dumbfounded as Ben squeezes my hand.

"That was erm, great Ben… and you Daniel, erm, well done," she says. "Let's try that again, and next time, erm Ben…"

"Yes?" he says, eyes wide open.

"A little less dramatic," she pleads, her voice calmer.

We both look straight at Adam; he is standing mouth wide open and staring right at us. He quickly closes his mouth, shakes his head, tuts, and walks away. This is what Ben meant when he said we would give him something to watch. This was a show alright, and Adam wasn't the only one staring, a small crowd had gathered.

"We did it!" Ben whispers, excitedly. "I don't think he will bother you again."

J D Baird © 2022

"He wasn't really bothering me."

"Well, you know what I mean," he shrugs.

We take our starting positions once more and I signal over to Ben to behave.

"Action!" bellows Amanda.

We dance again, Matthew kisses Elijah again, I feel warm inside, almost faint. I feel so close to Ben and dancing with him is like floating on a cloud.

"Great! says Amanda. "One more time, go from the final steps, leading into the kiss."

I don't think I could ever get tired of this, I feel lost in Ben's arms, I feel weak, I'm falling, hard. Matthew kisses Elijah for a third time today, but I feel *Ben*, and he knows it, he senses it too, this is real. This is identical to our first kiss, electricity flows through my veins and if it wasn't for the tempo in the music, I'm sure my heart would stop. Right here, right now. I'm lost in the moment. Ben holds me close, and I hold him. Our lips are dancing. I feel lightheaded, and I can no longer feel the floor. The music stops, resulting in the end of the kiss.

J D Baird © 2022

"I love you," I whisper, my eyes still closed.

"Not yet," Ben chuckles, "That's later."

"No, I love you, Ben!" I say again, opening my eyes and hearing the words leave my mouth. I love him.

"Cut!" shouts Amanda. "Perfect!" she adds as tears began to well up in her eyes.

Ben lets go of me and the people around us move on. He is standing completely still, looking at me.

"What did you say?"

"Never mind, forget I said anything," I say and swiftly walk towards the coffee.

'What the fuck have I just done?' I walk outside and take out my phone. I light a cigarette as I wait for an answer.

"I've only gone and told him!" I blurt out, pacing up and down. "I've ruined everything."

"Dan?" Stella asks.

"Yes, that's me! Dan, the complete idiot!"

"What? What have you done?" Stella gasps in horror.

"I told him I loved him, that's what!"

J D Baird © 2022

"And?"

"And nothing," I sigh, blowing out a huge ball of smoke.

"Places people!" I could hear Amanda screech from inside as she claps her hands. I throw my cigarette to the floor.

"I have to go!" I tell Stella.

"Call me later…" she says, and I cut her off.

I head back inside, and Ben is looking right at me. I look away in embarrassment and get into position. We learn a more upbeat routine and the entire time; I feel like the floor is going to swallow me whole at any moment. I can't look at him. What have I done? Why do those three words ruin everything.

At the end of the evening, I grab my bag and head to the door swiftly, without thinking, I leave alone and walk out into the carpark. My head is full of unanswered questions. Where do I go? Do I go back to the apartment? What now… for us?

"Daniel!" I hear Ben hurrying behind me. "Daniel for fucks sake stop!" he shouts. I keep walking. "Daniel!" I stop and turn around. "Where are you going?" he asks.

I don't know where I'm going, and I don't want to answer even if I did. I turn and continue to walk.

"Daniel, stop!" he commands, out of breath and puts a hand on my shoulder.

"If you would just stop for a second," he says.

"Why? Why would it matter?" I turn to him, and he takes a deep breath, he looks deep into my eyes.

"Because I love you too, you idiot! Daniel, I love you too!"

CHAPTER 16 – HE LOVES ME TOO

I wake up and focus my eyes, Ben is lied opposite me, he looks so peaceful as he sleeps, and I can't help but smile. My heart is bursting, and I feel so lucky to be here with him. I watch as the sun glistens through a crack in the curtains and rests on his day-old stubbled jaw. He is the most beautiful thing I've ever seen, and *he loves me*. I grin again and he must sense me watching him. He takes a deep breath and blinks a couple of times before he opens his eyes fully. He looks at me and smiles. He groans and without saying a word, he pulls me into him wrapping his arms around me tightly and squeezing.

"I love you!" he says, eventually.

"I love you too!" I respond, wriggling from his grasp.

"I really do Daniel; I knew from the very moment I laid my eyes on you." He says as he leans in and kisses my forehead and I close my eyes softly.

"Last night, was the best night of my life," I say as my eyes open.

J D Baird © 2022

"Mine too," he says as he kisses my lips this time.

"Rehearsals start at 9am today!" I warn him.

"Oh Daniel! Do we have to go?" he protests, rolling onto his back." I could stay here in bed with you all day."

"It's going to be a lot of hard work, Daniel!" I mimic him, remembering what he told me back in Sheffield. "All work and no play, Daniel!" I try to copy his voice and I laugh out loud.

"I don't sound like that!"

"Oh yes, you do!" I mock him again and he jumps up and pulls the covers from me and walks into the bathroom.

"Hey, grumpy!" I call. "Would you like a coffee?"

"Yes, please!" I hear him reply.

I pull on my trousers and head to the kitchen. I look at the mess we had left last night. Our clothes are laying everywhere, and there are take away containers on the dining table. Ben walks in, rubbing his eyes.

"Oh dear!" he remarks picking up my t shirt from the dining table and throwing it at me. We sit and drink coffee in the quiet, both extremely tired from yesterday.

J D Baird © 2022

"We better make a move," he says, tying up his hair and picking up the keys.

***

We arrive at the studio and begin to warm up. Adam is talking to Amanda, no doubt trying to change some part of the routine, or something. I watch as Amanda dismisses him and calls us altogether.

"Now we are only into our fourth day and it's looking great everyone. I can see how hard you are all working but we really need to keep up this momentum. I know many of you are feeling the pressure, so it's important that you really do sleep well."

Ben coughs loudly and looks my way. I chuckle quietly and glance back at him. I catch Adam looking up too and squinting his eyes my way. He's definitely onto us and it really annoys him that he can't prove anything.

I learn my solo routine today. My choreographer is positively patient with me. She guides me through the steps several times and I feel confident that I have it. Ben comes over an hour or so later with a Danish and coffee.

J D Baird © 2022

"How you doing?"

"I'm ok. Thanks, just what I needed!" I say, reaching out for the warm drink.

"Good! So, some of the others are heading to the pub after, you up for that?

"Sure, sounds good!" I reply.

"Ok, catch you soon," he says as he leaves to re-join his group. "…and Daniel?" he turns around. "You look *great*!" he winks at me.

After rehearsals, we head to the pub, it's a really nice evening. We sit outside in the breeze, around a large wooden table with a faded green parasol above our heads. As we drink, we talk about how well the rehearsals are going. I look around at everyone, and notice the bond between us all, we are getting along and becoming a 'family' as Amanda likes to call us.

At around 10.30pm we say goodnight and Adam watches closely as Ben and I leave together.

The walk back with Ben is nice. The air is fresh and cool. I facetime Stella to update her on London. She answers excitedly.

"Hey you!"

She is sitting in the flat, huddled in a blanket and binge watching some series.

"Hang on!" she says whilst she pauses the TV. "Hi Dan! Is Ben with you?"

"Yes! He's here next to me," I say, positioning the phone to get Ben in shot.

"Hi Stella!" Ben says waving happily down the phone to her.

"Hi Ben! I hope you're looking after Daniel?" she says.

"Of course, I am!" he responds, and I smile.

"How's everything back at the flat?" I ask.

"Everything is fine," she tells me.

"That's good!

"Got to go!" she says, desperate to get back to her series and she hangs up.

"I really care about her," I tell Ben as we hang up.

"And me? he asks.

"Of course," I respond. "You mean the world to me!"

J D Baird © 2022

"And how much do you love me?"

"This much!" I say holding his hand and continuing to walk.

"Is that all?" he asks, playfully.

"Is this better?" I say and push him against a shop front and kiss him!

A man bangs on the window and tells us to clear off. We run a few steps and stop to catch our breath. I can't stop laughing. I bend over to stop myself from laughing and try to regulate my breathing.

"I really do love you, Daniel." he says.

We walk the rest of the way hand in hand, stopping for a bag of chips on the way.

"You know what Ben?" I say eating my chips. "You haven't cooked once since we arrived."

"And you haven't cooked at all," he tells me.

"I will cook for you," I say. "What do you fancy?"

"Surprise me," he says.

J D Baird © 2022

We get back and head straight to bed, I feel my eyes close as soon as my head hits the cool, soft pillow. I feel a warm arm around my waist. *'I'm in heaven!'* I think to myself as I drift off to sleep.

CHAPTER 17 - I MISS HIM

"Fuck!"

I hear Daniel shout from across the room, I look up at him, he has a face full of frustration; he's been struggling with his solo dance, but I didn't realise it was this bad.

We suddenly find ourselves in the second week of rehearsals and the pressure is on. We have costume fittings tomorrow and then two more days of relentless practice until the weekend. The next three days will see us rehearsing in the theatre and I'm looking forward to seeing the set. It's going to be worth all the hard work we are putting in, once we are up there on the stage. I'm so excited to perform live in the West End, it's a dream come true, with mum and dad coming to see the show on Tuesday. I'm really looking forward to seeing the guys again too, they are coming for the finale on Friday night with Stella, Bernie and Chloe.

I really want to go over and comfort Daniel, but I leave him to it, I think I will only distract him, and his expression shows sheer determination.

I'm sat across the room from Daniel, with a few of the dancers, talking about going out to a club tonight because we have been working so hard and we feel we should let our hair down, all on the hush of course. If Amanda caught wind of this she would go crazy, she expects us to be sleeping, not having fun!

I can't take it any longer, I grab a fresh bottle of water from the table and head in Daniel's direction. He looks pretty annoyed, sitting on the floor with his legs crossed and counting steps.

"It's looking good," I tell him, handing over the water.

He takes it from me and wipes his forehead.

"Thanks!" he says. "I just can't get the turn, Ben!"

"You will!" I tell him. "I can help, but not tonight."

He looks up at me, puzzled.

"Daniel, we are heading into town for a bite to eat and drinks, so that should help you destress. Come on, grab your things, we are ready to go."

J D Baird © 2022

"I think I'm going to stay here a while," he says.

"Really?" I ask, concerned about him.

"Yes, you go without me," he urges. "I'll meet you later."

"Are you sure?"

This will be the first time we have been apart since arriving in London and the thought of being without him tonight feels odd.

"I'm sure!" he says, standing up and walking away, he begins to go over his steps again.

I study him, I want to hold him and tell him everything will be okay, I want to feel his body against mine. I want to tell him he's gorgeous, his posture is perfect, his arms move in the right direction and with elegance, then I notice what he's talking about - he misses his step.

"Dammit!" he blasts.

"Call me soon!" I shout in his direction, wanting to comfort him. "Don't overdo it!"

One of the other dancers call out to me.

"Hurry up Ben!"

I turn and face the group. I can't even kiss him goodbye.

J D Baird © 2022

'Missing you already' I think to myself as I walk out with the others, and I feel a strange pang in my heart. Maybe I should have stayed with him, helped him?

***

There are quite a few of us going out tonight, we are the wayward, somewhat naughty dancers, however many didn't come and have left to rest and get an early night. Rob, who plays my brother in the dance, puts a large arm across my shoulder as we walk, and he offers me a cigarette. I take it and feel around in my pockets for a lighter.

"Here!" he says, lighting it for me.

I take a deep drag and my thoughts return to Daniel in the studio. He will be fine, I'm sure.

We arrive at an Italian place, and I order a lasagne and a lager. *'Daniel would love this.'* I think to myself, looking down at my plate. I text him.

'Looking forward to you joining us later x'

The group are chatting happily around me, drinks clinking together, and the sound of laughter fills the restaurant. I join in the conversation, and I find it doesn't take long before I start to relax in their company.

After paying the bill, we leave and go for a few drinks in a small pub across the road.

"Fancy a game of pool?" Rob asks me, eagerly.

"Doubles?" shouts Jenny. "Me and Sarah will play against you."

Jenny and Sarah are part of the troupe but don't have major roles.

"Sure!" I say as I place some coins in the table.

Matt, who is part of the production team, brings over some more drinks and I take a sip of my pint. My head is already feeling fuzzy, but it tastes so good, and I feel great! Bon Jovi starts to play in the background, his songs are my weakness, so I get up and dance around the pool table, feeling rather tipsy now I pretend my cue is a guitar, Jenny and Sarah join in, using their cues as microphones.

"Come on!" says Rob and he takes the break at the table, potting the yellow. He takes another shot but no ball in the pockets this time. As Jenny lifts her cue for her turn I check my phone to see if Daniel has called or messaged but he hasn't. It's starting to get late, and I wonder where he is. He said he would join us. There is a missed call from Eric. I try to text him, but my eyes begin to blur.

"Take over!" I gesture to Matt, and I pass him my pool cue.

I head out into the beer garden and tap Eric's name on my phone. It calls and he answers immediately.

"Hi Ben!" he says.

"Hi Eric, I missed a call."

"You missed me?"

"No! I missed a call, is everything okay?"

"I'm fine," he tells me. "I took a walk down to the beach this afternoon and I just wanted to let you know."

"That sounds nice, how are your parents?" I question him, not really knowing why I called him back.

"They're ok, Ben. Probably getting sick of me by now. I was thinking about going back to the house soon. Maybe when you get back from London?" he says, and I shudder at the thought of him being there.

He must know that I'm with Daniel now, I haven't told him, but our Instagram pictures don't exactly hide it.

"Still another two weeks before I'm back!" I tell him, trying to put him off.

"How is London?" he asks.

"It's great!" I exclaim. "Me and Da.." I stop. "I'm really enjoying rehearsals," I continue. "I've made some new friends, in fact, I'm out with them now."

"Okay, Ben, sounds like you are having fun, I'll let you go!"

"Yea, okay, thanks! Bye Eric."

"It's been great talking to you tonight, I wish I could hear your voice more. It's better than text."

"Yea, I'll call you again, when I can," I lie, not really wanting to. *'Why did I make this stupid call?'*

I've been in contact with Eric by text message, keeping him at a safe distance but none of the others back at the house know and they would be mortified if they found out. Sid would definitely ask if I was crazy, he told me to ignore him! Daniel doesn't know either, and it kills me keeping it from him. I love him so much and I really don't want to mess this up. I've been deleting my texts from Eric and messaging him when Daniel isn't around. He has nearly caught me on a few occasions, and I feel so guilty. I know I need to be honest and tell him because there is nothing going on between me and Eric, I'm just not sure he will understand. I will tell him back in Sheffield, not now, I don't want to ruin what we have right now, here in London. We are living out our dreams together and Eric, well he is a nightmare.

I head back inside and join the others. The girls had won the pool game and I laugh loudly at Rob and Matt.

"You really wouldn't be celebrating if I had been playing," I tease the girls.

"Where's Daniel tonight?" asks Jenny. "Why didn't he come out?"

"He's tired," I lie, sipping my pint, knowing he's probably not coming now. "I did ask him."

J D Baird © 2022

"That's a shame!" she replies.

I take out my phone and text Daniel again, I get no answer.

"You two look good together!" Sarah blurts out and giggles immaturely.

"Oh, we do, do we?" I say with a grin. "Well, he is rather hot!" I laugh.

"Are you sure there's nothing going on between you?" she probes further, and some of the others look my way, Adam's eyes lighting up as the conversation becomes interesting.

"Of course not! We are professionals!" I slur.

"Professional liars!" says Sarah, laughing.

"And lovers!" adds Jenny, laughing even more.

"So, what if they are!" says Matt, looking at me, an air of authority in his voice. "They are doing an incredible job," his tone turns to sarcasm. "…and if it takes sleeping together to perform like that on stage, then so be it," he laughs hard, and everyone joins in.

I laugh too but Adam doesn't, which makes me laugh even more.

J D Baird © 2022

'We are good together!' I think to myself as I wonder where he is.

We stay in the pub a while; I'm starting to feel quite drunk now and feel it's time to head home. There's no sign of Daniel even though I sent him the postcode to say where we are. I squint down at my phone; he hasn't even read my messages. I begin to worry so I go outside to call him. There's no answer so I light a cigarette before heading back inside.

"We are moving on," says Rob. "Are you coming with us?" he asks me as I walk back in.

I look down at my phone, sod it.

"Yes!" I reply, pushing my phone into my back pocket.

I stay out until 2am and head back to the house. My head is spinning, and the ground feels softer than usual. I'm really angry with Daniel. I'm pissed and I stagger through the London streets, alone.

When I finally get there, I turn the key in the door and climb up the stairs, holding on to the metal banister. I try to be as quiet as I can, but I stumble and trip, ripping my jeans. I reach the door and try to open it. The chain is on, on the inside. I bang on the door. Quietly at first.

"Daniel! Open the fucking door!" I shout. "Daniel, let me in!"

He comes to the door wearing only his underwear and lifts the chain off the latch.

"Jeeze Ben! Look at the state of you!" he says, opening the door.

"Where were you?" I ask him, pushing past. "I've been calling you all night."

"Where were you?" he responds. "Ben, it's gone two in the morning," he says as he walks away from me.

He heads to the bedroom and climbs into the bed. I follow, my head spinning. I undress, getting my head stuck in my shirt in the process and get into bed with him.

"I'm sorry!" I say as I lie next to him. He feels cold.

"Forget it," he says and rolls away from me. I fall asleep.

CHAPTER 18 – SORRY

Today is demotivating in the studio, I just can't seem to get the steps right for this one dance. There's a turn I need to make which is extremely difficult and I want to get it right; I have to get it right! I want to make sure it's perfect for Ben, for Stella, for my mum and me. I've been working towards this moment my entire life; I can't mess up now.

I practice the steps over and over; I turn and twist my leg wrong.

"Fuck!" that hurt that time.

I'm determined to get this right, so I keep going.

After some time, I sit on the floor to rest, rubbing the back of my stretched-out legs. Ben comes over to check on me and he is holding a bottle of water, he offers it to me, and I take it. He knows me well and I feel comfort in his presence. It makes me feel good inside knowing he was thinking about me.

"I really want to get this right!" I tell him.

He tells me that I am working too hard and reassures me that everything will be okay, but I just need to take some time to relax. I take some encouragement from his words, but I know I must push myself, just a bit further, before I'm ready. Ben tells me that they are heading out tonight, I want to go with him, but instead, I decide to stay a while to practice.

"I'll join you later!" I promise him and he leaves.

I have all intentions of joining him, there's nothing I want more than to be in his company tonight. I get up and go through the routine again.

"Dammit!" I shout as I turn the wrong way.

A couple of the others leave too and eventually I'm alone. The studio is quiet, so I play the music loud. I go over and over and over the routine.

My legs are hurting like hell and I'm overtired, but I keep going. I dance my heart out and push harder than I have ever done before.

I got it! I got it! I manage to get the turn right; I look around and there's no one here. I do it once more to make sure. I run to my bag to get my phone so I can call Ben, my battery is dead!

J D Baird © 2022

'Fuck!' I think to myself. It was a lonely feeling; I had achieved what I wanted to tonight and the only person I wanted to share it with was Ben.

I head back to the house; I have no idea where Ben is but I'm sure he won't be long. I put my phone on charge next to the bed and climb into the shower. It's been a long night and I just want to sleep. After the shower, I lay on the bed and close my eyes.

I'm awoken by banging on the door, It's Ben. I look down at my phone, 2.17am. I climb out of bed and go to the door, he's drunk, really drunk.

He has the cheek to ask *me* where I have been, he looks a mess, his hair is dishevelled, and his jeans are torn.

"Where have *you* been?" I ask him and inform him of the time.

I walk away and get back into bed, I don't want to look at him right now. How could he do this to me? He follows and gets in to bed with me after struggling out of his clothes.

"Sorry!" he says, putting a hand on my back.

"Forget it," I mutter. I close my eyes and go back to sleep.

***

I wake up and Ben is snoring loudly, so I leave him where he is and go and make coffee. We need to be at the studio in half an hour or so. I think about waking him, but I leave him a while because he needs the sleep. I make coffee for both of us, and I take it in and place it on the bedside next to him.

"Ben! I made coffee," I say waking him up. "We need to leave soon."

I go and sit at the dining table and wait for him to come in. I don't understand why he wouldn't call me last night. When he eventually appears, I look at him, this isn't the Ben I know. His hair is untidy and tangled, he looks like he's been dragged through a hedge.

"Take a shower!" I tell him and he looks at me.

"What is your problem?" he asks coldly.

"Nothing," I respond. "We need to be there at 9am."

"Why didn't you come out?" he asks me, rubbing his head in pain.

He's clearly suffering from excessive amounts of alcohol consumption, and I don't even care, I have no sympathy for him. He made the choice.

"I needed to practice," I tell him. "Ben I… Ben..."

I was going to tell him that I got the turn, that I was elated and that all I wanted was him last night but instead I kept it to myself, he looked in no fit state for positive news. I finish drinking my coffee.

"I'm going to leave." I tell him instead and I stand up, hauling my bag onto my shoulder and taking the keys from the side.

"Now?"

"Yes, I say, "I'll meet you there!" I kiss his head. "Take a shower first!"

I head out of the door. When I get out onto the streets, I feel strange, we have shared this walk every morning. I take my phone from my pocket and unlock the screen. Then I see it, he had been messaging me all night, I didn't realise. I feel like a fool, I think about turning back but instead, walk slowly to the studio.

J D Baird © 2022

"No Ben today?" asks Matt. "You two usually arrive together!"

"Yeah they do," said Rob, chuckling.

What had these guys been discussing last night?

"Yeah, he should be here soon," I mutter, reading the texts again that he sent me last night.

He was missing me, and I didn't even turn up. My heart felt heavy.

I'm feeling quite hungry, so I go and put some bread in the toaster, I didn't feel like eating before I left because I was so annoyed with Ben. Adam is there, plating up croissants and fresh fruit.

"Hi Daniel," he says. "We missed you last night."

I sit with Adam, and we talk. He seems concerned that I didn't come out last night and he talks about Ben, a lot! There's a strange atmosphere but I convince myself it's all in my head.

The studio door creeks open and I look up to see Ben walk in, he has showered, his hair is still damp and falls across his beautiful face black shades cover his eyes. I feel a flutter in my stomach and a pang in my heart. I feel so guilty for not reading his messages. The cast applause as he enters.

"Here he is!" says Rob. "What a sight for sore eyes!"

He sits down next to me and Adam.

"Are you ok?" I ask him.

"I will be!" he responds.

"I'm sorry!" I say.

"What do you have to be sorry for?" he asks.

"I…"

Amanda interrupts our conversation. Just as well, Adam is within earshot too.

"Listen up people! Today, we are going to the theatre to rehearse and there's a minibus waiting for us outside, make sure you bring everything you need! We leave in fifteen minutes."

There's a round of applause along with some whoops of joy and excitement.

I sit with Ben in silence, he puts his hand on my leg and I put my hand over his, curling my fingers around and holding tight.

"I'm sorry," he whispers.

J D Baird © 2022

"Me too," I whisper back.

I lean my head on his shoulder, pleased that we're okay. Ben leans his head back and rests it on the seat, I imagine his eyes are closed but I can't tell through the darkness of his glasses.

We arrive at the theatre and go inside. It is breath-taking and there are gasps of approval from everyone.

"Almost as beautiful as you," Ben whispers in my ear and I smile.

We walk onto the stage and look out. It is incredible. I picture mum sat in the seats looking down at me, proud of me and giving me a thumbs up for Ben.

We are running through the show from the start today, and I know I will have to perform my solo dance, I'm so nervous.

"Are you ok?" Ben asks me at the interval.

"I'm fine!" I say. "I'm just a little bit concerned about my dance.

He is standing in front of me, and he lifts his sunglasses and rests them on his head. He grabs both of my hands.

"You will be fine! You have worked so hard!"

J D Baird © 2022

The bell rings for the start of the second half of rehearsals. It's going well, a few minor hiccups here and there, but nothing too obvious or unfixable. Amanda is sitting in the centre of the auditorium, making notes and directing the lighting people. It's time for a group dance, we all run on.

At the end of the dance, I'm left on the stage by myself, it's my turn. The music starts and I'm terrified.

I look out at Amanda, sat looking at me, papers in hand and I am instantly taken back to the first time I saw Ben, the feelings I had when he first looked at me, the electricity, the physical attraction and the intensity of the connection I felt with him.

Images of us run through my mind, the dog, our first kiss, the night he cooked and… and I'm suddenly at ease. I feel my heart beat along with the music and the notes carry me. I rise from my crouching position, and I run to the left of the stage, I make the leap and land softly, my hands are in front of my face as I sway from side to side. I step back and turn!

I hit every step and I am ecstatic. Ben runs on!

J D Baird © 2022

"That was fucking amazing!" he says quietly, picking me up from the floor, my chest rising and falling rapidly.

He leads me out into the wings, and he tells me again. "Daniel that was great, you looked perfect out there!"

"Thank you!" I say out of breath.

If only he knew, it was him that got me through it! There's another scene before we are back on stage, so we watch on, he holds my hand at the side of the stage. He doesn't care any longer.

J D Baird © 2022

CHAPTER 19 – ERIC CALLING

He did it! I couldn't have been any prouder of Daniel, he hit the turn like the step was made for him. I couldn't breathe watching him, I felt his nerves as though they were my own. He's worked so hard. I watch on as he finishes his dance, he looks so beautiful out there, so elegant, so damn good, I should pinch myself. Daniel finishes and I run on stage; I can feel his heart pounding in his chest, I'm so happy for him. We walk to the side of the stage together and I can't help but hold his hand. He's mine and I don't care who knows anymore, I love him, everything about him. I can't imagine my life without him now.

"Ready for our kiss, '*Elijah!*'" I ask him.

"Yes, '*Matthew!*'" he replies, and we take the stage eager to dance.

Dancing with Daniel is my new favourite thing to do. It feels as though we have always danced together, as though we were always meant to be. We go through it with no issues and the kiss never gets boring, however, it always leaves me wanting more, but as Amanda has warned me, I need to rain it in. So, reluctantly I do, I kiss Daniel like '*Matthew*' is supposed to kiss '*Elijah.*'

Rehearsals finish and we all head to the minibus to take us back to the studio. The slow strides we take show our fatigue. We are definitely looking forward to a well-deserved, day off on Saturday. I slump down, heavily into my seat. Back at the studio, we say our goodbyes to everyone and head home.

"Imagine if Adam was playing opposite you," Daniel teases me as we walk.

"Ha, ha! Well, how would you feel if you had to watch me kiss him?"

We both shudder in sync and laugh. I couldn't imagine ever kissing anyone else, ever again.

We reach the apartment and climb wearily up the stairs.

"Maybe we should have rented first floor?" Daniel says resting against the wall next to the door.

I lean into him and kiss him, and my phone vibrates in my pocket, Daniel feels it too.

J D Baird © 2022

"Was that your phone?" he asks me.

"Yes, I say!" moving away, unable to deny it.

"Aren't you going to see who it is?" he says opening the door.

I take my phone out of my pocket, unlock it and see a message from Eric.

"So, who is it?" Daniel asks innocently as he walks through the door.

"Just my mum," I lie, walking in after him, deleting the text and shoving my phone back into my pocket.

I feel so bad, Daniel deserves to know the truth. We head into the living room and we both collapse on the settee. We fall asleep there and then, drained with fatigue.

I wake up a short while later with Daniel's arm across my waist and his head on my chest. I look down at him.

"Daniel!" I whisper and shake him gently.

He lifts his head up.

"What time is it?" he asks me, so I squint at the clock to check.

"11.45pm," I respond.

He stands up and walks to the sink, he runs the tap a while before filling a glass with cold water. He turns and looks at me with his deep brown eyes, drawing me into his soul, I watch as he drinks. I feel every inch of my body ache for him. He is profoundly beautiful, and he can sense my intentions. He walks back over in my direction.

"Let's go to bed," he says as he holds out his hand in front of me.

I take it and follow him. Still holding my hand, he leads me through the door, once we are inside the room he stops still and lets my hand go. My arms fall to my side, and he turns to me, he moves close and kisses my neck. I close my eyes. The feel of his lips on my skin is a wonderful sensation and sets my pulse racing.

He stops. I open my eyes to see him facing me, I open my mouth to tell him I love him, and he places a finger on my lips

"Ssshh!" he whispers and moves his finger slowly, replacing it with his mouth.

I feel his hands on my waist, he grasps the bottom of my shirt and pulls it over my head, he kisses me again, dropping it to the floor. I reach out and find the top of his trousers and unbutton them. He takes a small step back and lifts his shirt, I watch as he reveals his lean body and defined outline. I take in his smell, the lust I feel for him is far greater now I'm in love. He lifts his top over his head, and it dangles from his right arm. He steps forward, moving both of his hands to my face and kisses me hard, the softness of his shirt touches the back of my head, and it makes me shiver as it falls from his hand to the floor, caressing my back on its way. The taste of him gets better with each kiss, the urgency of our passion makes Daniel stumble and hit the back of his legs on the bed. He sits down.

"You're beautiful!" he says looking up at me and I lean over to kiss him.

My phone starts to ring in my pocket, Daniel reaches his hand in, and I stop him abruptly, placing my hand over his tightly. He senses my panic and pulls out my phone. We both look at the screen. *'Eric calling'*

"What the fuck?" Daniel shouts, standing up and shoving my phone, hard into my stomach and I clasp both hands around his.

"Wait!" I ask him and he pulls his hands from my grip, releasing my phone.

It drops to the floor and the ringing stops. He turns away from me and buttons up his trousers, he picks up his shirt from the floor and puts it over his head, pushing past me he slams the door on the way out.

"Shit!" I pick up my phone, I immediately text Eric.

'Don't call me, don't text me, don't contact me again!'
'Why? What did I do?'
'I am with Daniel now, we are together.'

There's no response. I turn off my phone and throw it on the bed.

"Daniel!" I call out to him, opening the bedroom door and pulling my top over my head. He's sat at the dining table; I walk around and sit opposite him. He doesn't even look at me. "Daniel,

I'm sorry! I didn't know he was going to call," I say, which is a half-truth.

He just looks at me. I manage to convince him there's nothing going on and I blame Eric. I get up and walk round the table.

"Daniel, it's you I want, only you!" he looks so annoyed, and I can't help but feel crap, I know it's my fault, I know I should have told him right from the start.

I should have listened to Sid, then maybe I wouldn't have hurt Daniel like this.

"We should get some sleep!" he says finally, and he heads back to the bedroom, I follow without saying a word.

He takes off his shirt and trousers and climbs into bed. He turns and faces the window. I take off my clothes too and climb in next to him, I wrap my arms around him.

"You hurt me!" he says.

"I know, I never meant to," I reply, holding him tighter. "I'm sorry."

"Promise me you won't lie to me ever again."

J D Baird © 2022

"I promise!" I tell him.

I feel his body move up and down as he takes short breaths.

I can feel his pain and it hurts me too.

CHAPTER 20 – HOW LONG?

I wake up before Ben and sit up! I think about last night and it confuses me. Why would he keep it from me? He said there was nothing going on between him and Eric, but there must be, for him to stay in contact with him, all this time. He apologised but how can I believe him? How can I be sure?

Ben wakes up and looks up at me, we both get out of bed. We hardly speak over breakfast, and this scares me. Has something been going on with him and Eric? The walk to the studio is continued in silence until Ben speaks.

"Are we ok?" he asks me. '*No, we are not.*' I think to myself, my whole body tensing at the thought of him and Eric.

"How long?" I respond, ignoring his question. Of course, we're not ok.

"How long?" he asks looking up from the floor, staring out in front of us, daring not to look at me.

J D Baird © 2022

"Yes, how long?" I press. "How long has this thing been going on?" I yell, grabbing Ben by his arm and turning him to face me.

He could barely make eye contact with me, something which felt so natural before had become problematic for him.

"Since we left for London, maybe earlier," he admits.

I can feel my world grow smaller. The bitter pain of betrayal, rife through my body. I can't believe in the two weeks I have been forming a relationship with him, he's been hanging onto a toxic one. I'm livid at the thought of them! He told me that it meant nothing. He told me back in Sheffield that he didn't have feelings for Eric.

"Why?" I ask, releasing my grip from his arm.

I can feel my hands begin to shake, so I fold my arms across my chest to hinder my outrage.

"I don't know," Ben says sheepishly. "He's been in contact with me over text and I was worried about him, I guess."

'Worried about him?' I think to myself, but I can't bring myself to respond.

I continue to walk on, dissatisfied with his excuses.

"Daniel, talk to me!" he says catching up with me.

I refuse to talk, this feeling in my stomach makes me sick. I don't want to ask any more questions because I'm not sure I'm ready for the answers.

We reach the studio and go inside; I walk away from Ben and seek out Adam. He's pleased to see me. I chat with Adam a while.

It's final rehearsals today and I'm not in any mood to dance, I try but keep picturing Ben with Eric, was he with him the way he is with me? I torture myself thinking about it. Amanda can tell that I'm not putting one hundred percent effort in, and I keep getting screamed at. It has no effect on me, her words fill the air but not my ears. I watch as Ben goes outside for a cigarette alone. I couldn't care less; I hate him right now.

I continue talking to Adam, he's unaware something is wrong, and he is a friendly distraction for the moment, until Ben comes back in through the door and walks straight over that is, he sits with me and Adam and starts discussing it, there and then. I politely ask Adam to leave, so we can talk.

CHAPTER 21 – TALK TO ME

On the way into the studio, I confess to Daniel the contact Eric and I have kept up since Sheffield. It's somewhat of a relief to finally tell him, but his silent treatment worries me. I can feel the pain I've caused in the grip of his hand on my shirt and the tone of his voice. I can't bear to look at him, so I search the floor with my eyes.

Today isn't a great day, I feel like shit, Daniel hates me, and I hate myself. How could I be so stupid? We keep our distance in rehearsal as much as possible, this is Daniel's choice, and this hurts so much. I go outside for a cigarette, hoping he will follow. He doesn't. I sit on the step and my phone vibrates. It's Eric. I look around to check I'm alone before reading his message.

'Hi Ben.'

'I told you not to message me anymore.'

'I know, I just wanted to check you were okay.'

'I'm fine.'

'Good.'

'Look Eric, we are in the theatre next week and I can no longer contact you.'

'Just tell me one thing.'

'What?'

'Where are you playing and the times of the shows?'

'Why?'

'I'd like to keep an eye on the reviews, you're still my friend.'

I tell him where and when we are playing.

'Thank you Ben, and good luck.'

I immediately delete and block his number; I don't want him to contact me again. I realise that I made it worse by replying, but I worried about Eric, he was my friend after all.

I only care about Daniel now and I need find him and tell him just how much he means to me, that I made a stupid mistake, that he is the only one and always will be. I go back inside and see Daniel sat with Adam, so I join them. I don't hesitate my words.

"Look Daniel, I'm sorry," I say. "It didn't mean a thing; I've always told you that and that's the truth. I've never loved anyone as much as I do you." I plead with him to forgive me, and he looks at the floor.

"Is this another joke?" asks Adam looking at the pair of us puzzled.

"But why would you keep that from me?" Daniel responds.

He looks up and stares me dead in the eyes, I can see the hurt, his once bright brown eyes have turned cold and sad, I long for him to forgive me. It hurts so much.

"Come on guys, It's not funny anymore!" laughs Adam.

"I was worried about your reaction, I was going to tell you back in Sheffield, I swear." I say, ignoring Adam.

"My reaction?" he asks stunned and then he turns to Adam, "Will you give us a minute?" he asks him, politely.

Adam looks across at me, I nod at him, and he stands and then he slopes off. I watch as he joins a group of people he starts talking to them and pointing in our direction. That's the least of my worries, all I care about is the man sat in front of me. The man I fell for, the man I would do anything for.

"It's the truth!" I continue. "Please believe me."

"I don't know." Daniel says quietly. "It just hurts, knowing that you would keep that from me."

"I will never hide anything from you again, I promise." I say as I hold his hands.

He moves his hands away from mine and I feel a shiver of ice cut through me.

We finish the day early; Amanda has decided that we could all do with the time off. There are cheers from some of the cast as she makes her announcement.

"See you all Sunday!" she says.

As strict as she is, you can see the passion that runs through her core and I'm pretty sure she's only being cruel to be kind. She must have a soft side.

"Shall we go for food?" I ask him quietly. "Just the two of us?"

"I'd really like that," he responds, surprising me, looking back in my direction.

J D Baird © 2022

It wasn't the reaction I had expected, my heart skips a beat and I smile back at him through the biggest wave of relief. I know I have a lot of making up to do.

J D Baird © 2022

CHAPTER 22 – FOOD FOR THOUGHT

Food tonight with Ben was nice although I could still feel an irritating pang in my heart, throughout the entire evening, even though I could tell he was sorry.

When we arrive back at the apartment, I take some time to think about things. I want to forgive him, I really do. I lie on our bed alone and think about the unexpected whirlwind I've found myself in. Things are moving incredibly fast, and I realise I don't actually know anything about Ben.

When we met he had this thing going on with Eric, he told me it meant nothing, and I was so caught up in the moment, so wrapped in lust, I didn't listen to my head. Even Stella asked if I was sure. Now I sit here and question myself, I know I just have to trust him. I need to let it go. I remind myself that I have always been sensible, and this is the craziest and possibly the stupidest risk I've ever taken. I try to weigh out if it's worth it. It must be, my head tells me to run but I decide to go with my gut. I have never felt the way I feel, like the way I feel when I'm with Ben. When we dance together our hearts beat as one, I sense that I have always known him. I feel like he's a part of me. It may not have been that long ago, but Eric is in his past I tell myself, our past.

Ben promised that he would cut all ties with Eric when we get back to Sheffield, he told me that he had already deleted his number and blocked him so he couldn't contact him, the rest of the time we were in London. I call Stella for advice.

"Hi babe!" she answers.

"Hi Stella! I miss you!" I respond.

I try to find the right words. I tell her about last night.

"He's a dog!" Stella says annoyed.

I explain that it's not his fault, but it takes her a while to warm to this idea. She eventually settles down and stops threatening to come to London and rip his balls off! This is typical Stella, act first, think later, she makes me laugh out loud.

"Not long now!" I tell her.

"Seven days and counting," she says.

"I really can't wait to see you," I sigh.

J D Baird © 2022

"Me neither," she says.

She tells me all the gossip, Chloe and Sid are still together and getting on quite well, she has been meeting with Ben's friends and they all met in The Duke again last week.

"It has become our spot," she tells me.

This makes me happy, knowing that our friends get along. I think about the future I have with Ben and draw in breath.

"Dan?" Stella says.

"Yes?"

"Remember that very first time you saw him?"

"I do!" I tell her, thinking back to the audition, and recalling the electricity that sparked across the room setting my soul on fire.

"Hold onto that, it's all you need!"

"I know!"

"I love you Daniel!" her voice soft and meaningful.

"I love you more!" I say before hanging up the phone.

She's right, I tell myself. We have a connection like no other.

I walk into the lounge to see Ben sat on the settee watching T.V. I join him, neither of us speak, just sit there watching the box in silence. He puts an arm around my shoulder, and I welcome it. Our first fight and I hate every part of it.

***

We wake up late the next morning.

"Saturday!" I say out loud stretching my arms high above my head.

The mood has lifted, and yesterday has become a faded nightmare. I don't ever want to feel that way again.

"What shall we do today? asks Ben turning to me.

"I don't know," I respond.

"I have an idea," he says. "You should cook for me, you promised remember."

"So, I did," I say with a grin.

We get up and head to the shops, the great thing about London is just how close everything is.

"I'm going to make sandwiches," I tease, looking around the shelves.

"You better not!" he demands.

I search around for ingredients and Ben stops at the sweet counter, weighing out two huge tubs of mixed jellies and mallows, he eats a jellied-bean and tosses one in my direction.

"I love you!" he says.

"You too!" I say back.

We find teabags because his parents are coming next week. We walk a bit further and turn down another aisle, Ben spots some cereal and puts it in the basket.

"That's my boyfriend!" he tells an old lady, shuffling past with a shopping trolley.

I look up and gasp!

"That's nice dear!" she utters, and we both laugh.

I grab his arm, "Boyfriend?" I ask.

"Yes!" he says proudly. "Daniel Walters, you are my boyfriend and I want the world to know."

I walk off, every fibre of my being, chuffed with happiness. I find pasta sheets and mince; I walk down another aisle to fetch tomatoes and seasoning. Ben catches up with me and he puts his sweets in the basket as we head to the till. I start to place the items on the belt.

"Oh! I forgot something!" he says and walks towards the wine section.

He returns with a bottle of Italian red wine.

"I love you!" he whispers in my ear as he places the bottle amongst the pasta sheets and cornflakes.

"I love you too," I whisper back.

We pay and walk home, all the while the term 'boyfriend' circles around my head and I smile uncontrollably. Ben searches the bags that I am holding and takes a handful of sweets. He stuffs a few into his mouth and he shoves a large marshmallow in mine and laughs, I nearly choke, and he laughs more. I chew the sweet lump of sugar and he kisses me.

"Hey! Take one of these bags!" I say looking down at my arms, as I realise I've been walking, holding both bags, whilst he's been acting a fool. He takes one and we walk on.

It's so good to feel like this again, I remember all the things about him that made me fall hard in the first place. Aside from the fact he is undeniably handsome, he's a complete fool, full of energy, and most importantly, he makes me laugh.

We get back into the apartment and place the bags on the side, I empty them out and he helps. He picks up the pasta sheets.

"Lasagne!" he exclaims. "That's my favourite, how did you know?"

"I didn't!" I respond.

Ben goes and sits at the dining table, and I see him open his laptop, press the power button and stare at the screen, waiting.

"Are you working?" I ask him. "It's meant to be a day off."

"Not really," he says. "I just wanted to check my emails and see how the business is going."

I walk over and close the lid of his laptop.

"No!" I tell him. "That can wait. They will call you if there's a problem. Today is about me and you and nothing else." He grabs my shirt and pulls me down towards him.

"Okay!" he says kissing me.

"Now let me go!" I request as I take his hand off my shirt. "I have dinner to prepare."

J D Baird © 2022

I walk back over to the kitchen side and see Ben watching me, I open the mince and empty it into a pan. He eventually goes over to the settee and sits down, he flicks on the tv, the football is on.

"I didn't know you were a fan!" I say, stirring the sauce into the browned mince.

"I'm not as such," he replies. "I just like the way they kick around the ball."

We both laugh. I finish preparing the food and join him on the settee whilst it cooks. I look at the T.V. then look at Ben, he tilts his head to one side whilst pursing his bottom lip and raising his eyebrows, I look back at the tv to see what he's reacting to.

"I agree!" I say and he nudges me with his elbow.

We continue to watch the football and I have no idea what is going on.

"Shall I grab you a beer?" I ask, standing up.

"Oh no!" he says. "Open the wine."

When the food is ready, we sit at the table. I must admit it's nowhere as near as good as Ben's attempt. We start to eat.

J D Baird © 2022

"This is delicious, Dan!" he says with a mouthful of lasagne.

I look across the table at him and see his satisfaction in the meal, I try not to be too complacent but it's hard not to feel a little smug.

"Sorry, I didn't prepare the table," I say, a few mouthfuls later.

We finish and head over to the settee and sit back. We talk about next week and how exciting it's going to be on the stage, enthusiasm about the West End consumes us and Ben's eyes light up as he speaks. Watching him illuminate fills me with happiness.

"I'm nervous!" I admit to him.

"Don't be, you will be fine. I have seen how good you are out there, and the pressure will only boost your performance!" he says.

"Thanks!"

"Who is coming to see you?" he asks, looking at me eagerly for an answer.

J D Baird © 2022

I withhold from the question, my face turns pale, and my throat feels dry. I gulp.

"Dan, what's wrong?" he asks.

I search his eyes to be certain I can trust him. I can.

"Ben, my mum is dead!" I say bluntly.

I feel my body tense as the cold, dark words escape my mouth. "And my dad is a homophobic prick! So, unfortunately, I won't have anyone come and see me at the shows, only Stella."

Without a word, he holds my hands in his. I look down and feel comfort in his caress and my tense body begins to relax. I tell him in more detail about what happened the night I found my mum and the pain I felt at the time and ever since. He sits still as he listens. I continue to tell him that after mum died, I left home and moved to Sheffield because my dad couldn't cope with the fact that he had a gay son.

"I repulsed him, and he couldn't bear to look at me, he would call me the most horrific names which I refuse to repeat."

"That's awful, Dan, I'm so sorry."

J D Baird © 2022

I look up at him as he sympathises with me, his face crumpled with disgust toward my father. He stands to pour me a glass of wine and when he sits back down he picks up one of my hands, my other hand holding the wine glass, he holds it between his palms and lifts it to his mouth. He holds my knuckles to his mouth momentarily before gently kissing them. He replaces my hand with his own glass and takes a large sip.

"Dan, I need to tell you something too," he confesses.

"You can tell me anything!" I say, sitting up,

He takes a deep breath.

"I lost my older brother when we were young. He was hit by a car when we were playing outside. I had kicked a ball into the road, and he ran out, without thinking and.."

He stops. He places his glass on the coffee table and looks at me.

"It's ok! Go on," I say.

"It all happened so suddenly, so quickly!" he recalls the memory. "I didn't mean it. I should have stopped him! It was all my fault!"

J D Baird © 2022

He blames himself for the accident and I understand, I feel the pain that is going through his heart, just telling me is a huge step.

"It's not your fault!" I tell him sternly.

Even though I blame myself, every day, for mum, believing I could have done more, if I hadn't gone out that day, if only I had stayed with her, she would be here now. The guilt eats away at me knowing I could have saved her. I could have helped her.

"You see, that's why my parents are so overprotective. It's the reason why mum fusses over me so much, I love her so much, but at times its suffocating. That's why I left, I had to move out Dan, because I couldn't bear living with the guilt I was carrying and having daily reminders of what I did, what I took away from her." he blurts out.

I can see the sadness in his eyes. I pour us both another glass of wine and the red liquid runs out. We stare at the glasses in front of us not knowing what more to say to one another.

"But my parents will absolutely love you," he says, changing the subject, holding back his tears.

J D Baird © 2022

"I'm looking forward to meeting them," I tell him, as I use the back of my hand to wipe away the tear that is forming in my own eye.

The atmosphere in the apartment is heavy, so we decide to go out for a walk and sober up. Outside, the air feels cooler, and we walk off that gigantic meal. We talk to each other about why we dance and the peace it brings us, in our hectic lives. He understands me like no one else, not even Stella. Ben feels the same way I do and recognises that I dance because I lose myself in the music, I appreciate that Ben dances to feel free from the guilt and the hurt, we both dance to escape.

"Your mum would be so proud of you Dan, you are amazing," he tells me. "You are one in a million and I would be so lost without you," he puts an arm around my shoulder. "Don't ever leave me."

"I won't," I promise him, as we continue to walk, arm in arm through the cool London air.

J D Baird © 2022

CHAPTER 23 – FIRST NIGHT NERVES

It's the morning of the opening night, I open my eyes and look across at Dan. He's sleeping. He looks so peaceful as he takes in the air around him delicately before releasing it slowly through his nose. The room is quiet and warmed by the sunshine breaking through the open window. My heart is full of love for him, all I want to do is protect him now, I never want to see him hurt ever again. I feel like a new chapter has begun in my life, I've never told anyone my deepest secrets, but Dan is a part of me now, he is the rhythm of my life, he is the beat of my soul. He wakes. He looks at me, his warm brown eyes invite me in.

"Ben!" he calls out, stirring from his much-needed slumber.

"Dan," I respond, running my hand through his soft brown hair.

"I never want to wake up without you," he says.

"You won't," I reply, and I kiss his head. "Are you ready for tonight?"

"As ready as I'll ever be!" he replies.

J D Baird © 2022

We both reluctantly leave from the comfort of the warm sheets, shower and change. The curtain is at 7 pm.

We sit and have breakfast together, no need for words. Every now and then we catch a glimpse of each other but remain silent. I finish eating before Dan and stand to take my bowl to the sink, Dan looks up at me and I smile down at him.

We spend the rest of the morning lazing around the apartment, not really knowing what to do. We watch some daytime tv, smoke on the balcony and drink coffee. My mum calls.

"Hey darling!" she says, and I take a deep breath.

"Hello mum!"

"I miss you Ben."

"You too mum, how's dad?"

"He's good, he's here listening!"

"Hi dad!"

"Hi son, how are you feeling about tonight?" he asks.

"Ok, I think, there's not much more I can do, just have to go out and give it my all." I tell him.

"You will be great, Ben!" his encouragement is sincere.

J D Baird © 2022

"Thank you dad."

"We can't wait to come and see you tomorrow," mum chips in.

It dawns on me that I haven't told her about Daniel.

"I can't wait to see you either," I tell her. "Oh, and mum, dad, I've got someone special I'd like you to meet," I say, looking over at Dan.

"Did you meet a boy?" mum says excitedly.

"I did, we met in Sheffield, you were there!" I laugh.

"Oh my gosh, Ben! That cute little thing from your audition? I'll put my best dress on," she teases.

A bolt of happiness runs through me. I also know she's serious about the dress, whatever her tone of voice may suggest.

"See you tomorrow!" I say. "Bye dad!"

"Bye son!" they both say delighted.

Dan and I collect our belongings and head out for some lunch. Afterwards, we meet Rob, Matt, Jenny and Sarah and head to the studio together.

J D Baird © 2022

Amanda is standing outside, beaming with excitement. There's a ripple of joy running through the cast as we board the minibus, Daniel squeezes my arm and I feel as excited as him.

We get to the theatre and there's an army of makeup artists and costume people ready to attack us and transform us into character. Dan and I have our own room because we both have lead parts. We enter the room and I look around, there's a rail to the left with our costumes hanging on it, marked with labels, reading 'Ben Thomas' and 'Daniel Walters', a large table with a lighted mirror and two stools, directly in front of us, on the floor to the right of the room are large, square bags that look to contain make-up and hair products.

"We've made it!" I say looking at Daniel.

He goes and sits on one of the stools, he faces the mirror and I study his reflection, it's not the same scared face I saw back in the audition room, it's a face full of pride and courage. I see him differently now; I know what lies beneath his eyes. He spins around to face me.

"We sure did! he says, looking around the room.

J D Baird © 2022

Amanda knocks on the door.

"Ben, Daniel," she says as she walks in. "You will put costumes on at 17.30, make-up, promptly at 18.00."

She is carrying a clipboard that holds the running order, and she has a headset on, which she talks into, leaving the room.

"So that gives us an hour and a half, what are we supposed to do until then?" Daniel asks me, still sitting in the chair.

"This?" I say walking over to him and lifting his face to mine as I bend in front of him.

There's another knock on the door and it opens abruptly, I jump back from Daniel and face the door.

"Mic check!" says one of the technicians bursting in, wearing all black.

He takes a microphone from a pack and fits it over the top of Daniel's head, all the while Daniel looks up at me as I make faces at him. The man presses a button on a small black box which is attached to the microphone and a green light appears. He calls down a radio, sound check for Daniel. He then proceeds to speak into Daniels mic and a voice comes from his radio.

J D Baird © 2022

"Daniel's check, clear!"

He unwraps the mic and places it in a small box and labels it DW. He looks right at me, and I go through the same experience. Daniel raises his eyebrows in my direction as I sit down, allowing the technician to call down the mic. He takes it off and as with Dan's, places my mic in a box labelled BT. He leaves the room as swiftly as he came in.

"Where were we?" I say to Daniel, turning my chair to face him.

"About here!" he says pulling me towards him and kissing me.

"I knew it!" a voice calls out and we both look up. There, standing in the doorway is Adam.

We laugh hysterically.

"Oh! Hi Adam," I say greeting him, eventually.

"Nice of you to knock!" Daniel adds.

"Well, the door was open," says Adam. "Anyway, I came to see you both and see how you were getting on. Clearly very well! We have just had our microphones fitted in the other room.

Do you guys want to come out for a smoke? Matt, Rob, and some of the others are there? Wow! This room is impressive, you guys are lucky! And you two, I thought as much!"

"Breathe!" Dan urges Adam as he doesn't take a breath and we all laugh.

We go and join the others for a cigarette. Outside, everybody is hyped up. There really isn't long now and first night nerves are beginning to show. We head back inside and take a walk across the vast stage, looking out at the empty seats.

"I wonder what it will feel like, when there are people there!" Daniel says.

We take a selfie of this moment and I upload it to Instagram, all the usual hashtags, #livingthedream #dance #firstnightnerves #London #WestEnd and a couple of extras #love #boyfriend. I tag Daniel.

It's 5.15pm almost time to get dressed so we walk back to the dressing room. Daniel texts Stella and then puts his phone away. He stands directly in front of me, and we hug, tight.

"I'm proud of you!" he says.

J D Baird © 2022

"I'm proud of you too!"

The door opens again, and two women come in to help us into our costumes, I'm helped into black trousers and a loose black vest, my mic is fitted for the second time, this time with a little more care and consideration.

I look up in Daniel's direction and I cannot believe my eyes, his captivating beauty makes me draw in a deep breath and I exhale slowly. He's dressed in floaty grey trousers and a matching oversized top. He looks as handsome as ever, I fall for him all over again.

It's time for make-up and we sit on the stools facing the door, we keep getting told off by our make-up artists respectively for talking to each other. Once we are made up and they pack up, I look at Daniel's face, his hair has been slicked back and there's a black liner under his eyes, he looks irresistible. I look in the mirror at my own face. My hair has been tied up, and I have the same black eyeliner as him.

"You look…beautiful!" he says turning to me, once we are alone again.

J D Baird © 2022

It turns 6.45 pm so we head backstage as directed. As we approach, we hear the hustling and bustling beyond the curtains. Daniel holds my hand at the side of the curtain, and we peer through a small gap.

"It looks so full!" he whispers to me.

This is when I realise they are waiting for me, out there in the crowd all eyes are going to be on me. It daunts on me and it's too late, I am the lead.

***

The curtains open and the music starts, I know what I need to do. Daniel releases my hand and I enter the stage. I stare out towards the lights and the music starts; I begin to dance. Adrenaline is running through my veins and the eyes of the crowd fuel my body; I dance like I've never danced before.

As I exit, the crowd cheers loudly, it's a feeling like no other, I walk towards my fellow cast, still full of adrenaline as they run past me onto the stage for their part, Daniel is with them, I watch on, as the floodlights follow him.

***

J D Baird © 2022

The performance is a hit, the audience loved it, we received a standing ovation on the first night and everybody is elated. The minibus arrives outside to take us back to the studio. We walk home still on cloud nine, I run in front of Daniel and stop him walking.

"I can't believe it, Daniel, did you hear the crowd?"

"Yes, Ben, it was wonderful, I've never felt so alive! You were a star Ben; you really smashed every bit of your performance!"

"You too Daniel, you were amazing out there!"

J D Baird © 2022

CHAPTER 24 – MEET THE PARENTS

I leave Ben at the apartment to go and pick up some milk. Ben's parents are arriving today, so he has stayed behind to tidy round, ready to welcome them. I worry about what they will think of me, but I am distracted by thoughts of yesterday. I am still beaming from last night's show, the high of it all is still ringing in my ears.

I walk past a news stand and see Ben on the cover of a local London paper. 'Magnificent Matthew' I can't believe my eyes; I stop to read it again. I pick up the paper and buy a copy. I hurry to collect the milk, eager to get back and show Ben the paper.

"Ben, Ben!" I cry as I turn my keys through the lock and burst in. "You will never believe this!"

I stop dead in my tracks, his parents are here. In our apartment. I shove the paper under my arm and close the door with my foot.

"You must be Daniel?" his mum asks me.

"Yes!" I say, placing the milk on the side and running a hand through my hair.

J D Baird © 2022

"Just in time," Ben says as he switches on the kettle, winking at me. "Daniel, these are my parents, Pete," he turns to his dad. "…and Jackie," he gestures to his mum.

"Nice to meet you!" I say, holding out my hand for Pete, paper still under my other arm.

He takes my hand and shakes it firmly, when he releases, I throw the paper on the couch. I can show him later.

"And you too, Mrs Thomas!"

I hold out my hand and she flings her arms open and scoops me up. I'm taken aback at the embrace but the warmth it fills me with is indescribable.

"You must be so proud of yourself?" she asks me, letting go. "The both of you," she looks up at Ben. "Now where's that tea, Ben?" she says, ushering me down to the dining table and urging Pete to sit down too. "I want to hear all about it."

Ben joins us with four cups of hot tea, I take a sip, burning my tongue in the process, digesting in what is actually happening. *'I'm meeting his parents.'*

J D Baird © 2022

We sit and talk for a while before Ben reminds us that we need to be at the theatre at 4 pm, therefore we should make a move if we are to see as much of London as possible today. We have already arranged to have lunch on the Thames. I'm a nervous wreck around Ben's mum and dad as I think about my own parents, and I know Ben senses this.

"Dan can you help me find my shoes?" he asks pulling me into the bedroom. "Relax!" he insists as I stand by the window looking out.

"I can't Ben, I'm so worried that I'll be a disappointment."

"You? Don't be stupid, she wore her best dress!" he laughs. "She adores you!"

"Are you sure?" I say, turning around and walking back to him.

"Yes, now let's get back in there!" he says pulling his shoes out from under the bed and pushing me forward. In I go.

***

We take the Northern Line from Leicester Square and change at Kennington, before arriving at London Bridge.

J D Baird © 2022

We amble across the bridge as Ben's mum and dad take in the sights and make our way to The Riverboat where we have our lunch booking. A friend of Ben's mum had suggested the place, I look at the small floating restaurant as we approach. Such a great choice, it's idyllic.

"Oh, this looks amazing, boys!" exclaims Ben's mum, as we sit at a beautifully decorated table.

Green ivy and pink petals are scattered on a crisp, white table runner. In the centre of the rustic table, stands a beautiful, unlit candle in a wooden holder. I must admit, it does look nice.

Ben and his dad talk about the business, and I listen closely to their interaction I watch on as the bond between them radiates across the table.

"The Jefferson's have taken out a contract," Pete informs Ben.

"Wow, dad! That's great news! How did you know?" Ben responds.

His eyes light up in delight, not quite like the way he looks at me, but delighted all the same.

"I rang the office last week, to check in," his dad murmurs in confession.

"I had no idea, dad, haven't had a single opportunity to check my emails," he squeezes my leg under the table. "Haven't opened my laptop!"

"They are always like this!" his mum turns to me and rolls her eyes. "Ever since the boys were big enough to dig a hole, he had them planting seeds in the garden! "Look!" she says as she takes out an old photograph from her purse.

I look into her delicate hands at the creased and slightly faded photograph, I instantly recognise Ben, he's the smaller of the two boys in the image, the short mop of curly hair and intense green eyes are an instant giveaway. He is holding a muddy spade with a red handle. A very similar-looking boy is standing next to him with one arm wrapped proudly around Ben's shoulder and a sapling ready for planting, held strong in the other hand. They are posing in front of a freshly dug hole and they look so innocent, so happy.

J D Baird © 2022

Ben looks down at the picture too and I sense the unease in him through his body language. I squeeze his hand under the table to reassure him it's ok and I can feel his gratitude by the squeeze which is reciprocated.

"Let's order!" says Pete, he must also feel the tension looming in the air.

"Yes, let's!" adds Ben as he watches his mum fold the picture up lovingly and place it back in her bag.

The food arrives and we all eat joyously, it's incredibly fascinating watching Ben with his parents. The love between them is immense and the pride that they show for him goes beyond anything I've ever known.

***

We walk around London for a while and the time comes for me and Ben to head to the theatre. It's been such a great day, Ben's parents are great, so welcoming and sweet, I'm not sure what I was so worried about. Ben's parents have plans to visit Buckingham Palace before the show tonight and they are already booked into a hotel for the night.

J D Baird © 2022

"We shall see you tonight!" says Jackie.

"Take care, the pair of you!" his dad adds.

"We will, have fun!" Ben responds.

We say our goodbyes and Ben and I catch a tube back to the West End. We arranged with Amanda yesterday, to come straight to the theatre tonight, everything we need is there so no need to get the minibus with the others.

"They are incredible!" I reveal to Ben, referring to his parents, on the tube ride back to the West End.

"Thank you!" he says. "I am so lucky to have them, I know," he sighs, warmly.

We arrive at the theatre and the same comedic drama as yesterday unfolds; this time Adam knocks on our room door before coming in. He's accepted that we are together, in fact, the whole cast says they knew pretty early on due to our obvious, tell-tale facial expressions. They say they found it quite entertaining watching us, desperate to touch each other, not to mention the amount of cigarette breaks we took together, they tell us it really makes no difference, and they are happy that we're happy. Jenny pulls out a copy of the paper, the same one I picked up this morning, which is still sat on the couch back home.

"Look at this!" she exclaims.

Rob reads out an extract from the paper:

"Marvellous Matthew! Ben Thomas, a delight for the eyes, his exquisite portrayal of Matthew, descends on the West End with his equally outstanding partner Daniel Walters. Daniel's magical and tear-jerking solo dance as Elijah rivals those at the top level in the industry. An all-round outstanding cast and fabulous performance from all involved…"

The review gets everyone pumped for tonight and I blush as I receive pats on the back, even though I had already read it this morning, it still feels like a dream. I really had no idea that I would end up here, with these amazing people, after that immensely hot morning back in the Sheffield audition. I think back to Sheffield and Stella. I can't wait to see her.

***

J D Baird © 2022

The show goes well and after we take our final bow and change, Ben's parents come backstage to meet and greet some of the cast. Ben's mum mingles in with the other dancers as his dad finds a seat. Trays of champagne are offered round, to recognise the tremendous review we received in the paper.

"Cheers!" Pete says, tapping his glass on mine.

"Thank you for your support tonight," I tell him.

"I wouldn't miss it for the world," he says.

"What wouldn't you miss?" Ben asks, appearing at my side, putting an arm around my waist.

"You lad!" You were unbelievable, both of you!" he says looking at me too. I felt proud of myself, proud of how far I'd come.

We say our goodbyes to Ben's parents, and they head back to their hotel, they are driving home early in the morning.

"See you in a few days!" Ben says as he waves them off, watching them climb into a cab, tears rolling down his mum's face.

"You ready?" he asks me, and we climb on to the bus to take us back to the studio.

J D Baird © 2022

***

At home, Ben spots the paper on the settee which I had tried to show him this morning.

"And that's why you came in screaming my name in excitement this morning? You're great! You know that right?" he says hugging me tightly then kissing my forehead.

J D Baird © 2022

CHAPTER 25 – CURTAIN CALL

Last night went exceptionally well but tonight I did not get the turn, maybe I was overthinking it. I'm devastated and feel like I have let myself and the others down. Everyone has told me not to worry, but how can I not worry about something so big? Understandably, if it was during one of the group numbers, then I probably would get over it, but it wasn't, it was my solo and I messed up.

"You did great Daniel, don't beat yourself up about it," comforts Ben as I crawl into bed.

"But now I'm worried about the finale tomorrow, what if it happens again?"

"It won't, just have faith in yourself, you know you can do it!"

"Thanks, Ben!"

'Maybe I am being stupid.' I tell myself as Ben hits the light and jumps into bed.

"Last night tomorrow!" he says.

J D Baird © 2022

"I know," I tell him. "How are you feeling about it?"

"Pretty sad to be honest Daniel, it's been the best three weeks of my life, here with you."

"Mine too!" I say, curling into him.

***

We slept really well last night which must have been because of the cooler air. Waking up next to Ben is the best feeling ever. He strokes my face and I rub my head into his hand kissing it.

"Good morning, you!" he says.

"Good morning!" I reply, taking a deep breath before I sit up.

"Breakfast?" he asks.

"Oh yes please!" I say, pulling him towards me.

"No, actual breakfast," he says getting out of bed.

"Yes!" I say laughing and I get out of bed too.

I go take a shower whilst Ben is in the kitchen making breakfast.

After I wash my hair and face, I let the warm soapy lather run down my body. I climb out and wrap a towel around my waist, brush my teeth whilst looking in the mirror at my reflection and I try not to think about last night, but my mistake is haunting me.

I hear Ben in the kitchen, singing along to the radio, and making breakfast, so I go in and join him. I sit at the table in my towel, and he brings over freshly cooked toast and a steaming cup of tea. He sits down beside me.

"You will be absolutely fine!" he says sensing my anxiety.

"I can't wait to see our friends tonight," I tell him.

Stella text me this morning, asking if I needed anything, she is so thoughtful but there's nothing I need. She also asked how things were going with Ben. I told her that I couldn't be any happier and she agreed telling me she had never known me to be this way. I'm looking forward to seeing the others again too, and I know Ben is overly excited to see Drake and Sid.

I really can't believe we are at the end of the tour already. It has flown by. If it wasn't for the tiredness I feel right now, I would definitely do this for another week. There are rumours amongst the cast that it will be played around the UK next year which excites me immensely. I try to keep my cool, we still have another night to get through.

Our friends will be arriving in the next hour or so and Ben and I get ready to meet them at the station. It's cooler outside today, which is a relief, although I'm not complaining, the sun has done wonders for my complexion. Ben grabs his shades, and we head out of the door.

***

We see the 12.45 train arrive on time from Sheffield and they get off. Stella runs hastily in my direction and hugs me like a mad woman, I think I'm going to pop!

"I have never been prouder of you Daniel!" she squeals straight into my ear, then kisses me hard on the cheek.

"And you *Mr Benjamin*," she changes her tone, turning to him. "We will have words tonight," she walks towards Ben.

"Stella!" I gasp, pulling her by the arm, away from him. "She doesn't mean it," I apologise as he laughs awkwardly.

"Benjamin?" he whispers towards me, shrugging his shoulders and I laugh.

J D Baird © 2022

I watch on as Drake and Sid literally pick Ben off the ground in an embrace and almost carry him away. His face lights up with emotion.

"We have missed you, buddy!" declares Sid, excitedly as they put him safely back on the ground.

"Yeah, really stoked for tonight," adds Drake.

Ben and I give Bernie and Chloe hugs and we force small talk; he keeps his distance from Stella as she eyeballs him.

It's such a wonderful feeling, (despite Stella being way overprotective) walking out of the station. I feel on top of the world.

We find a place to eat and then we take a trip to the London eye, I've always wanted to go on it, despite my mild fear of heights.

I stand at the window and look out into the London skyline; all my dreams have come true. An excellent group of friends, a gorgeous boyfriend, the most craziest, best friend a boy could ever wish for and a fantastic future to look forward to. I take a mental note of the way I am feeling, this is something I will carry with me forever. I feel his arms around my waist, and I don't need to turn around.

"I love you so much," he whispers into my ear.

"I love you more," I say still gazing out of the glass.

The atmosphere behind us is joyful, there's a surge of noise as our friends are taking selfies and updating profiles, whilst I just live for this moment, right here, right now, just Ben and I.

The ride stops and we depart.

"That was absolutely brilliant!" says Bernie.

"It sure was," I say holding on to Ben's hand tightly as we walk to the tube station.

***

We leave the others in a pub across the road from the theatre and Ben and I head in for the last time. It's a surreal feeling. We go to our makeup room and talk about the day and the fun we had. I change out of my casual clothes and dress in my costume, I look over at Ben as he's having his make-up applied for the final time and a wave of sadness falls over me; this part of my life is ending.

J D Baird © 2022

"This is it!" he says turning to me and reaching out for my hand and I take it. "After this, we have the rest of our lives in front of us Daniel, and I couldn't be happier knowing I am spending it with you," he says.

This immediately changes my mindset. I shouldn't be sad; I should be excited. This is only the beginning, this is chapter one, we have a whole story to write, together.

***

We meet the rest of the cast backstage and form a huddle for the last time, Amanda joins us.

"You are all amazing! Make this the best one yet!" she insists as we all place our hands into the centre of our circle.

"On three!" calls Matt.

We bounce our hands together on each count before releasing them into air, waving them around and calling out "We've got this!" simultaneously.

I smile anxiously across at to Ben, and he smiles back, nodding his head, it's confirmation that I can do the turn. He knows my thoughts. He knows how to lift me up. A surge of adrenaline runs through me like a warm powerful river.

At the end of the show, the cast run on, just as we have every night, in turn. I take my place and run down the centre to take my bow and wait for Ben. I stand centre stage and hear a screech.

"That's my boy! Go, Dan!" I look up and see her, clapping frantically and punching the air.

I smile at her; Stella just can't help herself, she's loud, she's crazy but I wouldn't change her for the world. Ben immediately runs down to join me and Sid and Drake whoop and holla, loudly above the crowd too, Ben puts both hands to his lips and blows a huge kiss out to the audience before taking his final bow. We get a standing ovation and the noise from the audience is immensely deafening. It is the wildest feeling, everybody is elated, the show could not have gone any better! Did I mention, I hit the turn?

"I had every faith in you," Ben tells me in the dressing room as we change.

J D Baird © 2022

***

We meet our friends afterwards and they join us backstage. Matt has said they are more than welcome to join us for the after-party.

The club is a few streets away, so we take a walk over in groups, there's champagne on arrival and I take a glass and hand a glass to Ben.

"Cheers!" he says clinking my glass as the rest follow on behind.

"This is incredible!" says Stella as she walks in, her eyes lighting up.

There are a few resounding noises of appreciation from the others too. I must admit, it is overwhelming.

There are photographers, journalists and a couple of D-list celebrities here. I have never been to such an extravagant party before. I down my much-needed drink and I feel the bubbles fizz in my empty stomach.

"We should eat," I tell Ben, reminding him that the last thing we ate were burgers this afternoon.

We head over to the buffet, Stella's eyes pop as she takes a plate and fills it. I consider the enormous spread laid out in front of us and select a mixture of sandwiches, mini sausage rolls, and some savoury nibbles, to fill the small void in my stomach. We have a table with our names on. Ben Thomas, Daniel Walters and guests.

"Ohh, this is so fancy!" says Bernie, as she takes a seat, with a plate full of chicken wings, sandwiches and mixed salad.

The room resembles an award ceremony but instead of a stage to collect awards, there is a large dance floor. Looking around the room, the atmosphere is in full swing already. The cast are dotted around talking gleefully to family and friends. We sit and eat.

A man in a suit walks over to Ben and shakes his hand.

"That was an outstanding performance."

"Thanks!" says Ben, still chewing.

He takes my hand immediately after.

"And you were incredible," he says.

J D Baird © 2022

He introduces himself as a journalist for a paper and asks if he can write a story, we agree and give him a few words for his article.

"Oh wow, you two are celebs!" says Chloe once he leaves.

"Not quite!" Ben laughs.

A waiter passes with a tray of fizz, and we help ourselves. Stella takes two! I look around the room, the excited journalist is now talking to Amanda.

The girls go off to the dance floor and leave us at the table.

"So, what's the plan for you two big stars when we get back to Sheffield?" chuckles Drake. "Will you need an entourage?" he smiles.

"We haven't thought that far," I answer.

"I have!" replies Ben, looking at me.

"You have?" I ask stunned.

Drake and Sid take this as a cue to leave and the table falls quiet.

"Yes," responds Ben.

"Oh?"

"Daniel, I love you so much, I want to spend my life with you. You came into my life at a time I wasn't expecting, and I can't imagine my life without you now."

"Ben… I…"

"Don't say anything, just listen."

I sit, mouth open, I think my heart has gone into cardiac arrest.

"I'm not saying move in with me or anything like that, but I want us to be together, like really together. You mean more to me than anything."

I think my soul just fled my body. I take a moment as I feel my heart kickstart back into action.

"Ben, I feel exactly the same, I feel safe with you. I want to be with you too. I love you more than anything," I exhale.

"So that's settled then?" he says taking my hand.

"Yes!" I say, overwhelmed with happiness, I didn't think it was possible to love him any more than I do right now.

I look over at the dance floor and Sid and Drake have joined the girls.

J D Baird © 2022

"Shall we?" I ask him, still clutching his hand.

We step onto the dance floor and join the others, such a joyous feeling, every moment with him gets better and better. I feel like I am floating in the clouds.

After a couple of hours, the booze-intoxicated air begins to hit me, I feel dizzy, and my head is light. The room is spinning. *'Time to head back to the apartment'* I think to myself. I walk over to Ben and tell him I'm ready to leave, he's sat in a chair, hair flopped over his eyes and his gentle swaying from side to side tells me he's ready to leave too. We go and find the others.

"We are ready to leave," I tell Stella.

"Okay, we won't be long behind you," she says hugging me.

Ben says farewell to the boys and lets them know we will see them tomorrow for the train ride back.

We call a cab, it's not safe to try and navigate the underground in the state we are. As we climb into the back of the shiny black cab, Ben reels off the address, I fall back into my seat and fumble around for the seatbelt, but no luck. Ben reaches across me and helps me, his touch turns me on, his body across mine. I can't wait to get back.

"You're adorable," he tells me, and my head flops forward towards my knees.

My eyes begin to blur, the low grumbling noise of the engine and the movement of the vehicle makes my stomach roll. My head feels like it's flown off somewhere into outer space and there's a sharp cramping pain right across my abdomen. My mouth begins to feel watery, and I just can't hold it, no matter how much I try. The contents of the party come up through my chest and gush out onto the floor.

"Not so adorable after all," says Ben as we are thrown out into the dark street.

"I'm sorry," I say, holding onto him as he guides me for the rest of the short walk home.

J D Baird © 2022

CHAPTER 26 – THE BEGINNING OF AN END

I wake the next morning, place both hands on my head, and hold tight, the pain is excruciating.

"Good morning!" I force an eye open and see Ben sat on the edge of the bed.

He has brought me some paracetamol and a glass of water. I take the water and drink, my eyes still closed.

"Breakfast?" he asks!

"No, absolutely not! How much did I drink last night?"

"I'm not entirely sure, but you were wasted."

"Ugggghhhh, what time did we get home?"

"Much later than we should have."

"What do you mean?" I ask him, taking the pills.

"We walked; do you remember?"

And that's when the evening came flooding back.

"I was sick, in the cab," I recoil in horror!

"Yes, on my shoes too!"

"I'm totally sorry," I tell him.

"Honestly, don't worry about it," he kisses my head as I rub my eyes. "Take your time," he says. "I'm sure the others aren't up yet either."

"Thanks," I say.

"No bother," he says leaving the room.

I sit up and the room spins, *'I'm never drinking alcohol again.'* I promise myself, sipping the water from my glass.

About twenty minutes later, I make my way to the living room.

"Hey! How are you feeling?" Ben asks as I enter, feeling rather sorry for myself.

"Slightly better!" I tell him as I slump down at the table.

"We need to pack," he says planting a coffee next to me.

"What did I do to deserve you?" I ask looking up at him, thankful for the coffee. I look around the room and wish I wasn't ending the most spectacular adventure on a hangover.

"We should go for lunch with the others once we are finished here," he suggests.

J D Baird © 2022

I finish my coffee and head to the shower, I let the cold water splash over me, and I feel my body come back to life. The paracetamol begins to take effect as I step out onto the cork bathmat and wrap a towel around my waist. I head to the bedroom and dress. Just as I begin to throw my clothes into my bag, Ben walks in.

"You look so much better," he says, kissing my cheek.

"Thanks, I feel it."

Ben pulls his bag out from underneath the bed and starts to empty the wardrobe and pack his things away too.

***

We arrive at Camden Market where we have arranged to meet the others, they are sitting outside a food stall when we arrive, all donning shades and looking far worse than I did earlier.

"Hey, guys! How was the hotel?" Ben asks as we sit.

There are some inaudible grunts from the group.

"That good?" I ask, laughing.

We take some menus and place our orders.

J D Baird © 2022

"Stella!" Are you ok?" I ask her, she's face down on the table.

"I'm fine!" she mumbles, holding an arm in the air for confirmation.

"What are you eating?" I ask her.

"Coffee!" she replies.

"No food?"

"Not yet," she says. "My tummy is fragile."

"Just like Daniel's then?" Ben says taking my hand.

"I'm okay now!" I tell him.

"So, last night," Ben continues. "We were kicked out of the cab because some of us were drunk and disorderly and decided to throw up all over!" he playfully mocks me.

"You didn't?" says Stella raising her head, squeezing out a laugh.

"Guilty!" I say.

"We've all been there!" says Drake.

"Ha ha! Don't we know it!" I reply pointing at him and the group laugh.

J D Baird © 2022

After food, we walk to the tube station, it's time to make our way back to Sheffield. It's a bittersweet feeling, I don't want to leave this beautiful city, it's full of so many memories now but I'm really looking forward to familiar faces, places, and even work.

CHAPTER 27 – YOU CAN'T SMOKE DOWN HERE

We were standing on the platform waiting for the tube back.

"I love you!" Ben whispers across to me.

Oh, how I love him too, he was just everything I could have ever wished for.

"What time did you say the tube was?" asks Stella, peering over the edge of the platform.

"It's due in around four minutes," answers Ben.

"Ahh I can't wait to get back," sighs Stella. "Shall we get a takeaway tonight? Our place?" she asks us all.

There is a resounding "Yes!" from everyone.

"Takeaway and TV it is then," she says, lighting up a cigarette and laughing. "I just love you guys!"

"You can't smoke down here!" I warn her, reaching out.

She's standing directly in front of me, so I try to take the cigarette from her mouth. Stella wasn't the type of girl to follow rules, as we all knew.

"I know, I know!" she replies, taking another drag before stamping it out on the floor. She is wild, but we all love her too. Despite her anarchy.

"Here comes security, you're done for now," laughs Bernie as a shadow appears heading in our direction rather sharply.

I looked up and I see him, right there in front of me, coming at me with menace. Tall, blonde hair, *'Eric?'* I blink it can't be. I hear the tube coming down the track and look directly at Stella, she's too close to the edge.

"Eric!" I yell out loud "It is you!"

I feel a sharp hard shove in my side, and I'm thrown to the ground. My bag hits the concrete before me, saving me from pain. Ben is beside me on the floor and I look at him confused. I hear the tube go by and feel annoyed that we have missed it. My ears are ringing loudly, and I can hear screaming. Everything is happening so quickly. I shake my head and look up; Eric's arms are held out in front of him. *'He had tried to kill me.'* He had tried to push me onto the tracks. Ben had saved my life. I look over to Bernie, she is on the ground with Sid and Drake wrapped around her, Chloe stood stiff as a board with her hands on her head, and I look back at Ben. His eyes were dark and his face pale. I look around the platform. Stella? Where is she?

"Stella!" I called out to her.

Ben held me.

"Stella!"

Bernie is still screaming, I don't understand. Eric looks toward Ben, a haunting glare in his eyes, his face distorted.

"I'm sorry!" he says before turning and sprinting away, back down the platform.

'Why was he running? Where was Stella? Why was Bernie screaming? Where was Stella? Why was Ben holding me so tight? Where was Stella? Why was Eric sorry?'

"Where is Stella?" I yell. "Where is she?"

No one gave me an answer, the station fell deadly silent, and I could see strangers running in our direction, but I couldn't hear anything anymore, the realisation hit me, and I feel time slow down, I can't breathe, I am choking, my mouth is dry. I grip Ben by his shoulders and shake him forcing out my words.

"Where is she?" I say, a hushed, panicked tone to my voice.

"She's gone Daniel, she's gone," he says.

"No! What do you mean, gone?" Ben holds onto me as I try to get to my feet.

I'm powerless in his arms, I scramble and scuffle with him, but he won't release his grip on me. For the first time, I feel his strength and I want to break free.

"Let me go!" I cry

"She's gone," he repeats, still holding me down as I try to fight.

I repeatedly hit him, pounding his chest with my fists. He doesn't let go. My body goes weak in his arms. I feel sick, I can't see, it hurts in my entire body. I wail the most horrendous sound as I cling on to Ben's shirt, I burrow my head into the safety of his chest.

It was supposed to be me, not her. Not my beautiful, fun-loving Stella.

J D Baird © 2022

CHAPTER 28 – I CAN'T LET YOU GO

Looking over at Daniel fills me with immense joy and excitement about our future together. I watch as he talks to Stella, on the platform he is glowing with happiness.

"I love you!" I whisper in his direction, and he smiles back.

Stella decides to light a cigarette and Daniel tries to take it away from her, I watch as they playfight near the edge of the track, all I can think about is takeaway at Daniel and Stella's flat tonight, cuddling up to the most gorgeous man in Sheffield. I'm so lucky to have him.

"Eric!" I hear Daniel shout.

I look up and dangerously approaching Daniel, at speed is Eric. *'Why? How?'* I don't have time to question myself. I can hear the tube hurtling towards the station, and I can see Eric's intentions. He's going to kill Daniel. I can't let that happen, I rush forward and push him out of the way. We land on the stone-cold floor and the weight of Daniel hits my leg hard; it hurts but he's safe. I see the tube but can no longer see Stella, I know instantly what has happened. Bernie is making an almighty noise that fills the tunnels of the underground.

"Where's Stella?" he repeats over and over again. I try to tell him she has gone but he can't hear me. He's searching for her, and he tries to escape my arms. I use all my power to keep him safe.

"I can't let you go!" I tell him as he's beating my chest with his fists, sharp knocks which feel like bricks hitting me, but I hold on, tighter.

I promised him, I would never let anything hurt him again. I hold him down and I feel his body become limp in mine, he screams in anguish, and I hold him close. I place my shaking hand over the back of his head to shield him from the chaos. I can see members of the public running in our direction, offering help.

"I'm sorry!" I whisper, clinging onto Daniel.

Eric stands at my side looking down at me, his face is distorted; he has the arrogance to apologise before he runs.

My heart burns when I realise this is all my fault! Guilt sweeps over me like an avalanche. Stella is his best friend; she didn't deserve that. What have I done to him? How could I let this happen?

Tears roll down my eyes as I feel myself being pulled away from Daniel, so I hold on as paramedics take us away from the edge of the platform.

I look around and see blue lights bouncing off the walls of the subway, I see the others, they are being escorted away by police officers. Sid looks in my direction.

"I will call you!" he tells me as he places an arm around Chloe.

I watch as they walk towards the exit with Drake and Bernie. Bernie is wrapped in a silver blanket, tears rolling down her eyes. I take my phone from my pocket.

"Mum."

"Hello darling, are you on your way home?"

"Mum listen, there's been a terrible accident. I.." I lower my voice, aware that Daniel hasn't come to terms with the situation.

"What is it sweetheart? Are you okay?"

J D Baird © 2022

"I'm fine, but I need you to get dad to come here, to London. I will explain when you get here, I love you!"

I end the call.

"Ben?" I look down at him, so vulnerable, so lost.

"Don't speak Dan, I'm here!" I say holding onto him. "I will never leave you!"

J D Baird © 2022

CHAPTER 29 – NIGHTMARE

I wake the next morning in an unfamiliar room, I look around my eyes are hazy, and there's cold toast and a milky warm tea next to me. I sit up quickly.

"Stella!" I call out.

Ben appears at the door, he looks at me, his eyes are cold.

"You're awake," he says as he comes and sits on the bed, flinching in pain as he sits. He holds his leg.

"Mum and dad collected us from the station last night, we got back around 4 am, I haven't slept thinking about you," he says. His words are lost in my ears.

"Please tell me this is all a horrific nightmare!" I plead with him, grabbing his arm.

"I can't," he tells me softly as he puts both arms around me. "I'm sorry Daniel, I can't."

I cry uncontrollably into his chest as he holds me. The unbearable pain seeps through my blood to every part of my body, I feel his arms around me, but they offer little comfort.

"I will never let anyone hurt you ever again Daniel," he says as he holds me tighter. "I will take care of you. I love you so much."

I scream inside, I love him too. but he can't take away the pain, no one can. My world has fallen apart. I hold onto him.

"I have lost everything Ben; you are all I have left."

THE END

J D Baird © 2022

EPILOGUE

Eric sat in his old room with his phone in his hand scrolling through pictures of himself and Ben, his arm covered in bandages, his infatuation with Ben was out of control.

He had arrived at his parents' house in Cornwall after attempting suicide, back in Sheffield. It was the best place for him right now but he did not see it that way.

Opening up Ben's Instagram he saw a new picture, he was at the coffee shop, 'on a date.'

"I bet it's that guy from the party," he thought to himself.

His mum was outside the door with the doctor.

J D Baird © 2022

"He is deeply depressed and will need medication for a while to overcome this," the doctor warned her sternly.

Eric heard every word of the conversation and laughed to himself. "I'm not depressed."

He tried to call Ben but there was no answer, so he sent him a text message. Eric truly believed he was fine, and that Ben would take care of him when he got back to the house.

Over the next few days, Eric contacted Ben by text, he longed to hear his voice but had to settle with text messages because Ben didn't answer the phone. Eric convinced himself that Ben was busy with work.

"Good morning, Eric" his mum sang, as she walked in and opened the curtains.

"Let's get some light in here," she said as she opened the window too. "Eric, it's hot in this room, do you fancy going for a walk? We can go down to the beach?"

He looked down at his phone and saw a picture of Ben out on another 'date' with Daniel and this repulsed him.

J D Baird © 2022

"No thanks! I'm fine here," he said with his eyes glued to his phone screen.

He watched him on Instagram, checking for updates, daily and he kept himself informed over what, where, when, and who Ben was with. His uncontrollable fascination was growing sinister by the hour.

Eric sent a message to Ben to tell him he felt better and that he would be coming home soon. He asked Ben if he missed him but Eric thought knew the truth.

"Of course, he doesn't miss me, how can he? When he's picking up cheap booze with disgusting Daniel, after yet another day out together."

The images of Ben and Daniel eat away at Eric and night after night he tormented himself. They looked so happy together, it was Daniel's fault, Daniel was taking him away, he thought to himself. He tried to call him, he just wanted to show Ben how much he loved him and that *they* could be good together. Eric wanted Ben and nothing was going to stop him, he was not prepared to let anything, *or anyone* get in his way.

J D Baird © 2022

That night, Eric called Ben and his phone was switched off. 'It's never switched off,' he thought to himself. 'He must be with Daniel again.' He tried again the next morning and once more he didn't receive a reply. This made Eric bitter with jealousy.

"Why is he doing this to me? We are best friends."

A couple of days later Eric received a phone call from Sid, Sid asked how he was, and Eric told him he was fine. He truly believed he was sane. Eric asked Sid about Ben, but Sid told him he must get over it and he should give Ben space.

"Ben is seeing Daniel now, they're happy and that's just the way it is," Sid had told him.

Eric couldn't take it, reeling with anger and hatred towards Daniel, he ended the call.

Eric took note of when Ben left for London and text him every day, sometimes Ben would respond which gave him hope but more often than not, his messages would be ignored.

This fuelled Eric's passion to hurt Daniel. With Daniel out of the way, he could get to Ben.

J D Baird © 2022

He studied a picture of Ben and Daniel on Snapchat; he saw that they were now a couple, and he was repulsed. He called Ben over and over and finally Ben responded.

"He's drunk," Eric thought to himself.

Hearing Ben's voice gave Eric a glimmer of hope, this was all he had wanted, he was now sure that they would get together when Ben returned from London.

Just as Eric started to believe there may be potential for him and Ben, he saw another picture on Instagram.

He was furious and called Ben around midnight, Ben didn't answer but instead Ben text Eric. Ben told him he no longer wanted to be a part of his life. This infuriated Eric further and he hatched a menacing plan to go to London, he could no longer wait for Ben to come home. He must see Ben as soon as possible. He had to change his mind.

He managed to get the details he needed from Ben, through deception. "I'll give him one more chance!" he thought as he packed his small rucksack.

J D Baird © 2022

He tried to call him over and over again, but his number had been blocked, so he logged into Ben's socials again and tracked his movements. He saw that they were in the theatre together with the hashtag 'boyfriend', Daniel was meeting his parents, this sickened and overwhelmed Eric. Worst of all, he was there in London with *their* friends on the London Eye.

Eric felt like he had lost everything, he blamed Daniel. He couldn't take it any longer, his mind was made up, he was going to London. He would have Ben.

Eric risked everything and left. He hated Daniel and he swore he would get rid of him, whatever it took.

He arrived in time for the final show, he watched on, hidden at the back of the theatre as Ben kissed Daniel on stage, it enflamed him, and he felt his blood begin to boil. He left the theatre before the final act. He knew he couldn't be seen, not yet. He watched from a distance as the group left and headed towards a club, he followed secretly behind.

He watched as they went in but there was no way he could go in too. He knew Ben and Daniel were living somewhere not too far from here, so he began to walk, towards an area last updated on Ben's Snapchat.

Sometime later, by sheer luck, he saw them walking together, Daniel was drunk and taking advantage of Ben, he had to stop him, and he followed, slowly in the shadows.

"Daniel is revolting," he told himself.

He stalked from behind a tree as they went inside. Eric left and booked himself into a B&B where he stayed awake throughout the night, planning to be at the apartment building again early the next morning.

He arrived outside, plotting something severely sinister, he watched as they left and followed them from a distance to Camden Market.

"How can they do this to me? Why are they leaving me out?"

Afterwards, he followed them into the tube station. He was going to kill Daniel; he was prepared to do whatever it took to have Ben back. He followed them onto the platform and seized the opportunity, he ran towards Daniel. He pushed out as hard as he

J D Baird © 2022

could, pushing him onto the tracks before the oncoming tube. That's when it happened. He missed. Ben had saved Daniel. *Ben loved Daniel.*

He was shocked, he didn't mean to hurt Stella, she was innocent, he wanted to destroy Daniel. Eric fantasised that with him out of the picture he would be with Ben. He instantly regretted his evil actions as he saw the look on Ben's face, he ran, he had nothing.

The next day, Eric found himself on the lonely streets of London, hiding away from the police, he had walked through the night. Eric was two days sleep deprived and couldn't take it any longer, he walked to London Bridge and climbed up to the edge.

"If I can't have Ben I don't want anyone," he told himself as he sat tentatively on the edge, looking down at the water below.

He felt a strong hand grip his shoulder; he looked up. "Come with me, young man!" He stood up, knowing his fate. He felt the sting of cold metal wrap around his wrists as he was led away…

Printed in Great Britain
by Amazon